THE LIGHT SEARCHER

SUSAN DANKER

THE LIGHT SEARCHER © 2024 Susan Danker. All rights reserved. No part of this book may be used or reproduced in any manner whatsoever without written permission except in the case of brief quotations embodied in critical articles and reviews.

This book is a work of fiction. Any names, characters, companies, organizations, places, events, locales and incidents are used in fictitious manner or are fictional. Any resemblance to actual persons, living or dead, actual companies or organizations or actual events is purely coincidental.

Mark, you are my light.

Kelsey and Ashton, you two have been my greatest teachers. Were it not for the two of you, I could not have written from the heart about the ability to fall in love with a child.

Lane, I wrote the book.

Melody, thank you for placing everything where it's supposed to be.

CHAPTER 1

Ben Sandrick didn't ride a horse. All six feet and four inches of his muscular stature became an extension of the graceful animal to work in one fluid movement. His easy sway with the horse's sudden shifts as they worked the cattle had me in a trance when his voice saying my name jerked me back. "Beth, I need you to hold them back from this gate while I gather these others!" I nudged my horse toward the gate and nodded, "Yep! I got it."

I've heard others describe Dad's eyes as arctic blue with a stare that could scare anyone into submission. Gramma told me once that he wanted to serve in the war, but she forbade it and insisted he stay to work the ranch. She wondered out loud to me if Dad had ever really forgiven her for it. I bet he would've risen in rank fast if he had enlisted. I watched him when he needed to get the upper hand on the ranch help and those men were tough. None of them were a match for Dad, though. I never witnessed him abuse his authority and he was always fair, but I can't recall a time that someone bucked him either. I always wondered how he gained that kind of respect and I wanted to learn. I practiced staring into the mirror at night with my own blue eyes that everybody said were just like his, determined to master that cool confidence and get the "I mean business" part mixed in just right like he did. It's that look that makes me think he would've been a great Captain of the U.S. Cavalry if Gramma would have let him go. I've been on the receiving end of the stare a few times myself, but Dad added in a little softness when he pointed his eyes at Dylynn or me in discipline. I knew when I could push back, but I'd also learned when not to cross the line. Dad was good like that. He could let people know his boundaries without having to tell them where they were.

Our place in Cherry County was where I wanted to be for the rest of my life. I loved everything about ranching—working with the horses and cattle, the quiet mornings riding fences, the smell of the hay field. But what tied me to it most was doing it all beside Dad. He shared his passion and knowledge with me in every chore, and I soaked it all in so that one day I could take over if he'd ever let me. We rode into the barnyard and took care of the horses before we headed to the house. There was a wagon at the fence by the house. "We better clean up a little, Beth. Looks like there's company for supper."

CHAPTER 2

Grant Richards and his son, Cal, were already at the table with Mom, Dad and Dylynn when I sat down for supper. Mr. Richards was a tall, barrel-chested man with a thick golden moustache. His eyes were kind and I liked him on sight. Cal was a younger version of his father with a trim waist and wide, muscular shoulders. His hair was lighter, he was bronzed from working in the sun and he had his dad's kind eyes. My stomach did backflips when Cal shook my hand in introduction. I hoped I was hiding it well, but Dylynn was biting back a grin and winked at me when we sat down to eat.

Dylynn was born two years after me and had Dad's light hair and blue eyes—the same as mine. Poor Mom, both Dylynn and I looked just like Dad. Neither of us got her jet-black hair or bright green eyes. Dad teased her when people commented on our traits and told her she was just an incubator. Mom insisted she was carrying a boy the minute she knew she was expecting Dylynn. She and Dad never considered choosing a girl's name because Mom was adamant the baby was a boy. When the baby arrived a girl, Dylynn had already stuck so Mom had the doctor spell the name with two y's on the birth certificate to lend it some femininity. Regardless of all the pink Mom decked her out in, there were always questions about why she'd been given a man's name. We didn't care what others thought, though. We were all so in love with her. Even though I was still a toddler myself when Dylynn arrived, Mom says I referred to her as "my baby" from the first time I got to hold her.

It was a contradiction that Dylynn carried the masculine name and I'd been given the name Beth. Dylynn preferred to be at Mom's side in everything. When I wanted her to ride out checking fences or counting pairs, she never wanted to go. She thought my pants looked uncomfortable and adored all her pretty dresses with the flowery patterns. She had a knack for creating the most amazing flavors in the kitchen and helping Mom with the ranch books, but she could handle a horse better than most of our walk-on hands when Dad needed the extra help. Dad believed we should be able to choose what we wanted. Beyond a healthy respect for everyone pitching in when necessary, Mom and Dad were fine to let me be out with the cattle and allow Dylynn free reign in the kitchen. Not only that, she had a natural ability to handle the ranch books that bordered on obsession. Her specific way of ordering the files took the task away from all of us when none of us could maintain the records in Dylynn's style. As time passed and we grew into teens, Mom and Dad mostly checked Dylynn's books for approval more than a need to make sure there were no mistakes. With Dylynn, mistakes were unacceptable, so we all gave up and let her take over. Fine with me. I would just as soon be outside than cooped up in the office that was tucked away under the stairs.

My attention came back to the conversation when I heard Dad mention the Texas cattle law. This subject had been the topic of conversation around the ranch for weeks as news filtered in about what the Kansas legislature planned to do to prevent sickness from entering the state. If the law passed, it was going to affect our way of life on the ranch and Dad was trying to figure out how to prepare for what may be ahead. Tonight's discussion didn't carry the heaviness of uncertainty like the talks Mom and Dad had been having. In fact, they were both jovial and Mr. Richards seemed almost giddy as he pitched his plan.

"Ben, Seline...we can do this and now's the perfect time. Omaha's going to need the help if they shut Kansas down and Ogallala's position on the Union Pacific's railroad map is the ideal location for the Texas drives. They can come right up the eastern side of Colorado to avoid Kansas and we'll load them on the railcars to Omaha just as fast as they can bring them! If we don't do this right away, someone else will get the jump on us. I have the land near Ogallala. I just need you to plan the stockyards and help me get it off the ground."

The smiles were big as Mom and Dad exchanged looks. "What do you think, girls? Do you want to join us in this? It'll be an investment of our money and we'll have to move, but I want it to be a family business." Dad's eyes were dancing, and I knew he and Mom had already decided. I loved this ranch and never thought anything would call me away from it or tempt me to leave, but the idea of doing something this adventurous stirred my spirit. I wasn't sure Dylynn would have any interest in leaving and I was afraid she'd balk if the decision came down to her agreement. I figured her wrong though, and she spoke up before I had the chance to say a word. "I'm all in, but only if I can handle the books!" Everyone nodded. I imagine they expected her to require control of the office like she'd taken over here at the ranch. I took a deep breath and looked Dad in the eye with mock seriousness, "I'm in under one condition. I wear pants when we're working. I know you said I could only wear pants when we're here on the ranch and I had to be dressed like a lady for town, but I'll have to be a lady in pants if I'm in on this. I don't want to be in the office doing bookwork. I want to help build it and I want to be on my horse when the cattle start coming through. Deal?"

With a sigh, Dad looked away for a moment as if he was torn. He reached under the table and came up with two gift boxes.

Holding one with a lavender ribbon out to Dylynn and one to me, he said, "I didn't think it would be any other way for either of you. Your mom and I had these made for you in hopes that tonight would be a celebration." My eyes questioned Mom and Dad as I accepted my box and set it in my lap. I looked across at Dylynn and waited for her to tear open her box. Cal and Mr. Richards smiled with curiosity, and Mom said, "Open them! It's this or no deal, so you both need to agree now or Mr. Richards and his son will have to find other partners."

Dylynn's gift was a leatherbound ledger and pencil box full of freshly sharpened pencils. She traced her hand over the gifts like they were the finest pearls. My box had a black satin bow. They wrapped my gifts with black bows ever since I claimed it was my favorite color when I was seven. It was an inside joke between us. I slid the bow off the box and removed the lid. Nestled in tissue were two new pairs of riding pants with doeskin inserts sewn on the seat and inner thighs. They knew! They knew we'd say yes, and they knew we'd each have our own conditions. Settling the box on the table in front of me, I stood up with my hand outstretched to Mr. Richards. "You have a deal, Mr. Richards!"

An eruption of hearty laughter from Mr. Richards warmed my heart as he stood to accept my handshake, "Your parents warned me you were firecrackers. Partners!" When he released my hand, Cal stepped in to replace his father's grasp with his own. His grip was firm and professional, but his eyes were communicating something very different when they looked into mine. He shook my hand and said quietly as if he and I were the only two people in the room, "I am looking forward to our partnership, Beth." What was probably only a few seconds felt like a frozen moment in time as I returned Cal's gaze, and then I was brought back by Dad subtly clearing his throat before asking Mom what we were having for dessert. Cal's polite handshake with Dylynn didn't go unnoticed by me as Mom passed out plates of angel food cake with fresh strawberries.

Later that night when I was alone in my room, I congratulated myself for staying planted on my feet both times Cal had grabbed my hand. The spark from that touch went straight to my gut and I thought my knees were going to buckle. "Cal Richards." I whispered his name. There was double meaning in the way he murmured the word partnership. The last thing I thought before I fell asleep that night was whether or not our deal was going to end up having double meaning for me, too.

CHAPTER 3

Building the stockyards became a labor of love we all committed our hearts to. Word traveled like wildfire to cattle owners in Texas that a new cattle town was in the making and the Sand-Rich Stockyards of Ogallala became well known before it was ever completed. Dad and Grant hired every man who was sober enough to show up for work each daybreak, and the progress was steady. We planned to be accepting cattle by summer and we were on track to meet our goal.

With all the good things came some challenges, though. Dad and Grant were well thought of among the people of Ogallala and the jobs the stockyards created were a boon to some of the families who had fallen on hard times, but there were a few who felt threatened by our industriousness. Jealousy created some problems with the simpler minded men who thought money should fall in their laps rather than be worked for. They could've been rich if they'd put as much effort into working an honest job as they did trying to ruin us. One day, a stray ranch hand wandered in looking for work and he'd had too much time on the bar stool before he gutted up to ask for a job. Cal and I were working on the pens and could see the drunkard confronting Dad. Dad politely shook his hand and visited for a bit. When I saw him shake his head no for the second time in response to the man's requests for work, I saw Dad's jaw clench. The next move the drunk made was a misplaced jab with a rusty pocketknife. Loosely missing his aim for Dad's throat, the filthy knife blade went into Dad's shoulder. Dad had him on the ground with the knife thrown out of reach before anyone could get close enough to help. At the sight of Dad's clenched jaw, Cal had hopped the fence rail and headed toward the tussle at a dead run, but the blade was already out of Dad's shoulder by the time Cal got to Dad's side. As Grant ran up, Cal and Dad were already dragging the drifter toward the front of the stockyards to have the sheriff take him off to a jail cell for a night of sobering up behind bars.

With the excitement over, we all got back to work. Dad dismissed any concern we had over his wounded shoulder and went inside the office to have Mom tend to it. Dad worked on under Mom's close watch while he wore his arm in a sling and seemed to be healing fine, but the long days' efforts in preparing the stockyards for summer started taking their toll. He struggled to get through the day without needing to rest for a few hours in the afternoon and he started going to bed early in the evenings, which was totally unlike the night owl father I'd grown up with. He always told us his body didn't require much sleep and that he stayed awake most of the night to make sure his girls all slept safely. To see him surrendering to a weariness outside his control was hard to watch and we were all worried. Mom fussed over him, and Grant and Cal begged him to take more breaks. Dad's midnight naps and before dawn wake ups turned into early evening slumbers that sometimes lasted well into the late morning hours. Mom insisted he eat more, and Dylynn tried tempting him with new creations she invented in the kitchen. The rest of us enjoyed her efforts, but Dad could only take a few bites before he would have to leave the table to collapse back into bed from exhaustion. Concern and confusion plagued us. How could this commanding presence in our lives be diminishing while we watched helplessly?

As the days took the weight off Dad's physique, he couldn't hide it. His clothes hung from him and often his color wasn't good. He'd punch another hole in his belt to cinch his pants tighter on his shrinking waist, give us a wink and claim he was shedding pounds to get back to his "fighting weight." He kept pushing, though, and insisted he would rally once the summer sun started healing whatever it was that ailed him. Dylynn and I were in the kitchen preparing to start our day one morning a few weeks later when we heard Mom scream. We tore into their bedroom to find her holding Dad's too still body in her arms. He'd passed in his sleep sometime in the night and

Mom woke to find him gone from us. I stood frozen in place, unable to form words, cry or move my body. Dylynn sat down by Mom and placed a comforting hand on her back, but she was oblivious to our presence. A keening sound erupted from her and I could hear her faintly saying, "No, Ben. No. We were supposed to go together. You can't leave me here to live without you." I don't know how much time passed; me standing there frozen in a shocked numbness, Mom begging Dad to come back and Dylynn holding on to Mom.

Realizing we were with her, Mom sat up and told me to go get Grant and Cal. I was beginning to rock back and forth as I stared unbelievingly at Dad's body. It's strange how our minds can't accept or comprehend what our eyes are seeing. This couldn't be. Dad was young and healthy. How did he just waste away right in front of us in such a short time? How can there be no twinkle left in his eyes or smirk on his face? "Beth. Honey, you need to come back to us. Beth." Mom was standing in front of me now. How had she moved from the bed? "Beth." Swimming up to the surface, I recognized Mom's eyes looking into mine and her hands on my shoulders. Tears were streaming down her face, but she was in complete control of her voice when she asked, "Can you hear me, baby?" I pulled out of my stupor and a sobbing flood escaped me as I fell in a heap at Mom's feet. Leaving her vigil beside Dad, Dylynn joined Mom to help gather me up off the floor. Situating me on her vanity stool, Mom held my hand while she spoke softly but firmly, "Beth, we have a lot of tears to shed over this man that loved us. It's going to bend us over in pain, but he wouldn't want it to break us. You need to go get Grant and Cal. Can you manage it while Dylynn and I try to get things in order here?" Nodding, still not trusting myself to speak, I stood up and left the house without looking back at the bed Mom would never sleep in again. I didn't need to see it again. The image of Dad's lifeless form would be burned into my mind for the rest of my life.

CHAPTER 4

Doc liked to read medical journals. He was a fascinating man who was thought odd by many in town. I thought he was an amazing intellectual, and I always appreciated his exciting conversations about the latest medical information he'd learned. We visited often, so he was comfortable talking to me about his ponderings over Dad's sudden death. He thought Dad died of a bacterial infection that had traveled to his heart from the knife wound. He explained that the dirty knife blade probably introduced the bacteria into the bloodstream. Although Dad's wound healed, the bacteria stayed in the body and attacked his heart.

We discussed it outside after Dad's funeral. I would share Doc's opinion with Mom and Dylynn later after everyone left. Right now, they were accepting condolences from all the stockyards help and townspeople. Grant was with them, and Cal stood on the porch watching me like he was waiting for my next collapse. I knew he was worried, but his intense stare that tracked my every move was knocking me off center. I needed to focus on what we were going to do about the stockyards opening now that Dad was gone. I needed to talk to Dylynn about where we stood financially. I wanted to make sure Mom was going to get through the days ahead of her without Dad. I did not need to be thinking about what would become of Cal and me right now. I pushed it out of my head. I silently ordered the thoughts to go away. There was no time to think about myself when Mom and Dylynn needed me to be focused on our future.

After waving at Doc as he left the yard, Cal eased off the porch and headed my way. Caring nothing about the eyes of everyone else on us, he wrapped me in his arms and pushed my head to his chest. "Shh, Beth. I don't have anything to hide from these people. I love you. I'm not going to watch you falling apart on the inside and not do all I can to help hold you together. I'm going to be right here for you." Setting himself away from me a bit, he laid his gentle hand on my heart and said, "And, I want to be in here too. Please don't push me away because you think you have to be strong for Seline and Dylynn. Dad and I are still your partners. We want you to stay with us at the stockyards, and we're going to do all we can to keep this moving forward to honor Ben's dream." I gathered myself and explained, "Cal, it's just that right now…" He stopped my rambling with "Right now, we're going to thank God for the time he gave us with your dad and you're going to lean on the ones who love you. That's all. We'll figure out tomorrow and the next day when they get here." Words couldn't pass through the choked up tears, so I buried my head in Cal's chest and held on.

CHAPTER 5

Mom woke every morning and battled through the days with an iron will. She faced the meetings with the bank to settle Dad's business and spent long hours with Dylynn in the office making sure everything was intact with the books. Dylynn didn't need Mom's supervision, but she welcomed it knowing Mom needed the distraction. Dad and Mom had been wise with their money and there was enough set aside for the stockyards investment to finish building. Staffed with a full crew, the Sand-Rich Stockyards processed the intake and shipment of over 200,000 cattle by the end of their first year of business. The Ogallala cattle industry was booming, Sand-Rich was a well-known name among Midwestern ranchers and we loved every minute of the hard work.

Grant watched out for Mom and was the best friend he could

be to her while she grieved over Dad. Many evenings, Grant's horse would be patiently standing outside Mom's house while Grant took a stroll with Mom. The townsfolk assumed they would marry since they were both widowed, but Cal and I knew they would never be more than friends. Grant never loved another after Cal's mother passed years before we became partners, and Mom would never look at a man the way she had Dad. We were so glad they had each other to fill their loneliness, but Grant and Mom were halves of the people they'd been when their spouses were living. Those halves wouldn't be whole again until God called them home to reunite with their only loves.

As time is known to do, the ache in Mom's eyes started to dim and she became quick to laugh again. We could mention Dad without a stricken look passing over her face and now she'd smile wistfully when we shared memories of him. Our home became our gathering place for fun meals and games, and none of us would turn down an evening of Dylynn's good food. Fall was starting to give us mellow red and gold leaves on the trees and the drive season would soon come to a close. It would be time for our family to rest and plan for next Spring so we were all feeling celebratory.

Mom's apple trees were bursting with fruit and she enlisted all of us to come for picking. While Dylynn chose the best ones for pies and started filling the kitchen with smells laced with cinnamon and cloves, the rest of us picked until Mom announced we were out of room in the root cellar. Grant came up from taking his last load to the cellar, proudly showcasing his discovery—the old croquet set—and the competition was on. The spiced apple aroma mixed with the rich beef simmering on the stove wafted out into the backyard while we teased each other about what horrible croquet players we were. The day passed with that lazy perfection only crisp, sunny autumn days can provide and we were all ravenous when Dylynn finally called us to the table. We stuffed ourselves on beef stroganoff, roasted brussels sprouts with bacon and caramelized acorn squash. The cabernet sauvignon bottle was replaced more times than we could count, and the pink-gold sunset suspended us in its warm dusky glow. Then, we grumbled about where to make room in our stomachs for the still-warm wedges of apple pie Mom served with coffee for dessert.

After supper, Cal and I walked down to the stockyards to check the pens for the night, and we were almost back to the house when Cal tripped. I nearly fell over myself from laughing at the calamity of arms and legs as he went sprawling out in front of me. The wine was still thrumming through us, and we couldn't hold back the snickering as I tried to help him back to his feet. On his knees, Cal had one foot under him to stand up when the grin left his face. Grasping my hand, he held it to his heart and slipped a ring on my finger while he stared straight into my soul. "Beth Sandrick, marry me." I dropped my chin to my chest and closed my eyes. "Beth? What's wrong? Please don't turn me down. I've waited until I thought this was right, but I've wanted you since the night you bargained our partnership with your demand to wear pants! There isn't anyone else for me. If you say no, I will live the rest of my life alone and wish for you in my prayers every night before I fall asleep." My shoulders shook with mirth. I hated that I couldn't quell the laughter when he was so torn by my silence, but I was still trying to stifle my giggles from his fall and steady myself for this moment I wished would freeze in time. I looked down on him with my most solemn face and asked, "You think the pastor's still accepting callers at this hour? I don't want to wait, Cal."

We moved into the apartment for buyers that we'd added above the stockyards office while we decided where we wanted to live. It wasn't much, but Gramma always used to say a woman didn't mind sweeping a dirt floor when she was in love. Now, I knew what she meant. I loved our little space, even if it did carry the faint smell of the cattle outside.

CHAPTER 6

Our daily routine didn't change much since Cal and I had been working side by side for so long. Having the nights and mornings with him made me long for shorter workdays so we could be alone together in our little apartment. After supper one evening, Cal went out to do a last check of the cattle before we turned in for the night. I often watched him from our window that overlooked the pens as he rechecked gate latches on the pens. I was so proud to be his wife. I loved watching him move. His strong, athletic body was still a wonder to me.

Nearing the end of the last alley, Cal's back was to the tree line that bordered the back side of the stockyards. My trance was broken by the two eyes I saw reflecting out of the edge of the trees. I ran for the rifle we kept in the closet and threw open the window. The mountain lion was quietly stalking Cal and his lithe bulk was already in the same alley with Cal by the time I set up for a shot. I dared not holler Cal's name for fear of initiating the cat's attack, so I focused on steadying my breathing and remembered all of the things Dad told us to do when we had to make a shot under duress. I had to make the shot. I knew it would upset the cattle and I prayed the pen gates would hold. As the cat crept closer to Cal, the cattle erupted in warning. Cal turned just as the cat hunched down to leap at him. I released my deep breath, squeezed the trigger and it fell before it could come out of its crouch.

Cal whipped around to look up at me with awed confusion on his face. Reloading the gun while I ran, I tore down the stairs and out to the pens where Cal stood. He was leaning against the pen rails with shock in his eyes. "How did you make that shot, Beth? He would've mauled me. I never heard him. It's so dark out here. How, Beth?" Breathless, I told him, "I saw his eyes in the tree line. When he stalked out of the trees, I got the gun out of the closet in case he was going for the cattle. I never dreamed he'd come after you. When he turned in the alley, I knew it was you he was watching and not the cattle. I could see his eyes reflecting. I put my scope right between them and shot." Now, standing next to Cal, my nerves kicked in and my legs gave out as I sunk to the ground trying to dispel the thought of what could have been had I not been standing in the window watching Cal. With trembling hands, I set the rifle down and dropped my head in my hands. Cal kneeled and took my hands in his. "I'm alright, Beth. You make that shot cool as can be and now you lose it?" I shoved back at him playfully, "Don't laugh at me. I act first and panic later. Cal, it could have been over." He pulled me to his chest and shushed me gently, "It could have been, but it's not. I'm okay, Beth. Let's go get a horse to drag this thing out of here and get him buried. Man, did you know they stunk so bad? That is horrid. It's like a cat, but…" I interrupted him with my own mirth now, "Mountain sized?" He touched his forehead to mine and we stayed there a moment laughing with each other. The relief was flowing now and we were getting our bearings back.

After disposing of the big cat and taking a bath to get the stench off us, we snuggled up in bed. The adrenaline spike had worn off and we were both wiped out. Cal whispered, "I knew you could handle a gun, but how did you learn to shoot like that, Beth?" I smiled into his chest. I loved hearing the pride for me in his voice. "Dad insisted Mom, Dylynn and I be crack shots. Growing up on a ranch, he wanted all of us to be able to pick a coyote out of the herd if he wasn't there to handle it. We shot cans off fences for practice until Dad was satisfied that we could all protect the cattle, or ourselves if it came to that. I had a knack for it and enjoyed the sport of it so I hunted with Dad. We didn't need much venison since we had beef cattle, but we loved pheasant."

Cal rolled to his back and clucked his tongue in mock seriousness, "You think you know a person, you marry them and then find out they're a sharp shooter. What else don't I know about you, Beth?" I patted his chest and yawned, "Oh, time will tell I guess."

CHAPTER 7

Cal's childhood friend, Matthew Bishop, had joined us as an investor and proved himself a worthy cattleman. The flaming red hair and deep jade eyes were a testament to his Irish parents, and he stood eye to eye with Cal in height. Time and his loyalty finally won me over, but Cal and I weren't originally on the same page about having Matthew join us as a partner. Even though Matthew had an easy manner and a ready grin, an unsettling feeling made me question his motives. I didn't have a reason for it, but I sensed a foreboding darkness in him. I wanted to keep the stockyards business just family, but Cal persisted and he really did need the help. Cal's reassurances each time we discussed Matthew eased my wariness. He beat us to the yard most mornings and never shied away from the hard work that was never-ending to keep things in order around the stockyards.

It was Dylynn who finally convinced me to agree to Matthew's partnership after she and I misjudged him over a misunderstanding. They'd been spending hours together going through the books each week and Dylynn said she'd never met a person with an affinity for numbers like Matthew had. Other than herself, of course, she'd added with a wink. They pestered and picked on each other while they worked in the office and I wondered if there was a spark kindling between them, but Dylynn scoffed when I asked and swore she had no feelings for the man. Their relationship was strictly professional and she intended to keep it that way.

Business was flooding into the office one morning and Dylynn had a lot of interruptions from ranchers coming in to finalize their cattle sales. She and Matthew had counted the cash in the safe, agreed everything was balanced in the books and Dylynn planned to make a deposit at the bank that morning. With the rush of ranchers wanting their checks so they could get back on the trail for home, the deposit was left for later until the hustle slowed in the office. At lunchtime, Dylynn had sent the last man out the door and was unwrapping her sandwich when she noticed the door to the safe was ajar. She opened it to find no cash and dread turned her mouthful of sandwich to sawdust. Calming herself, she went in search of Matthew. Surely, there was an explanation for the missing money. She pleaded with God that it wasn't long gone. When I saw her approaching in a quick stride, I knew something was off. She came straight to me and told me and asked if I'd seen Matthew. I hadn't. Cal was on the other side of the yard up on the catwalk overlooking the pens and I hollered to get his attention. He ran to us and climbed down the stairs closest to us to ask what we needed and shook his head when we told him what we'd assumed of Matthew.

Matthew rode out that morning to meet a drive that needed help bringing in a herd. He'd been gone for hours. There was no way he took the money. Cal was sure it had been one of the ranchers or hands that must have slipped by Dylynn while the office was full of people. She was adamant that no one had gotten behind the counter and she and Matthew were the last people to handle the cash. Cal looked disgusted with us and turned away. There was fire in his eyes when he looked back at us. With his anger just barely controlled, he hissed out through gritted teeth, "Matthew did not take it. I won't hear another word from either of you. I'm going to tell the sheriff what happened and we'll get some men gathered to follow the groups that left this morning. I'm telling you, it wasn't Matt!"

"What wasn't Matt?" Matthew's voice hit us as he sauntered up to see what the three of us were huddled up about. He had overheard Cal's words. Dylynn turned to him with fury in her eyes and asked, "Where's the money, Matthew? We counted it when we balanced this morning and you were the last one with it before the rush hit. The safe's empty and you've been gone all morning. How do you walk up like you don't know what's going on?" He raised his eyebrows in shock, sighed and bit the side of his cheek as he reached for his back pocket to produce the bank deposit slip. "I knew it was going to be this afternoon before you'd be able to get to the bank with that line of ranchers out the office door. I took the cash out in my saddle bags and made the deposit on my way out to meet the drive when I left this morning. You thought I...?" Matthew left the sentence unfinished with a crushed look. "Oh, Matthew," Dylynn groaned. "I'm to blame for this. I jumped to conclusions instead of asking and then blamed you when I told Beth what happened. Cal defended you, but I was so mad I wouldn't listen. I'm not used to having anyone handle things but me and I guess my trust is pretty weak for people not related to us." Inhaling deeply and setting his shoulders to his full height, his clenched jaw setting his face in hard angles, Matthew stalked away from us. He mounted his horse and loped out of the yard. At the gate, he headed out of town at a full gallop. Dylynn and I looked at Cal as he stared after Matthew. We waited for Cal to put us in our place, but he said nothing. There was no warmth in his eyes for me when he looked down at me—only disappointment. He turned and walked away with a quiet calm that scared me. I knew he loved me, but I didn't know how I was going to make this right.

After an uncomfortably silent supper, Cal left the table with polite thanks for the meal as if he were speaking to a stranger. I cleaned up the kitchen and went outside for a walk on the catwalk above the pens to settle my mind. Also, to pray God would tell me how to fix the damage Dylynn and I had done. While I was up on the catwalk, I saw Dylynn moving toward the yard from town at a slow pace. It looked like I wasn't the only one taking some night air to think through my actions and accusations. I joined her on the street and we walked for a while with only the cattle's soft lowing serenading our thoughts. "Beth," Dylynn started tentatively. "I never know if I should respect the silence when I can tell you're thinking about something or if I should speak my mind. I'm feeling like I should speak my mind so I hope your head's in a place to hear me without getting prickly." I smirked; as much at myself because I knew I could be prickly when people tried reasoning with me before I was ready and at Dylynn because she knew me so well.

She drew herself up, I guessed to fill her lungs with the courage to spit it out, and said, "I know Cal wants to make Matthew a partner and I know you've had your reservations about it. Maybe you feel like the timing isn't right but maybe it's perfect because we need help around here. Grant and Mom need to ease out of things. They're tired and we can't do it all. I think the apology you're figuring out how to give Matthew tomorrow would go a long way if you followed it with a partnership offer." Her body slumped like she'd just unloaded an anvil off her back, but I knew she was waiting for me to fire back at her about mentioning the partnership. Looking up, I sent a silent thank you to God for answering my prayer through Dylynn and then hugged her to me. "Being my sister has to be a tough job and I'm sorry I make hard talks even harder sometimes, but I agree. I prayed God would help me figure out how to fix what we did today, and this is it. I've been so bullheaded about keeping Sand-Rich in the family, but Matthew is a good fit. First, I need to go back to Cal and fix this with him. Then, I'll see if he thinks now is a good time. I'll let you know in the morning and maybe we can take Matthew to lunch to get this resolved. Good night, Dylynn. I love you."

Cal had his back to me when I climbed into bed. "Cal, I know you aren't asleep. Be mad at me. I deserve it, but I hope you'll hear me when I tell you how sorry I am for accusing Matthew. I will apologize to him tomorrow. I know that doesn't just wipe away how badly Dylynn and I messed up today, but I want to show him how sincere I am about being wrong. Do you think it would be a good time to ask him to sign a partnership agreement?"

CHAPTER 8

Cal surprised me with land he'd purchased and I loved it at first sight. There was a clear creek running through the quarter he'd chosen and a natural meadow on the rise right above it. The spot was just waiting for someone to build a house on it, and we were anxious to have our own place. We worked at the stockyards during the day and spent our evenings doing all we could to hurry the house's finish. I wanted to be moved in before I started showing because I knew Cal wouldn't let me do anything once I told him it wasn't going to be just the two of us for much longer. Keeping my secret from him was torture, but I wanted to be in our home when I gave him the news. It was a girl; I was already sure of it. Only three months along, I was already calling her Hannah.

Dylynn would have known I was expecting because she was

usually so in tune with me, but she'd been blessedly distracted. His name was Captain Evan Ross. After Evan's enlistment was up, he visited Ogallala to see the stockyards. Following a tour from Cal and Matthew, Evan offered to buy lunch. The men discovered Evan had a talent for breaking horses and asked if he'd be interested in staying on to help with Cal's and my latest idea for a branch of Sand-Rich Companies. As much as Cal thrived on being a cattleman, horses were his first love and we'd discovered we were good partners at breaking colts. Cal bought me a palomino filly and we gentled her together. We enjoyed it so much, we started throwing around the idea to add a side business at the stockyards. He'd been working on some corrals near the stockyards and planned to sell saddle broke horses. With all the cowboys and cattlemen visiting, it seemed like a smart move, but Cal didn't have any extra time to develop a string with the demands of the stockyards and building our house. Evan shook on it and Cal took him to the office so Dylynn could set him up on the payroll.

Dylynn watched the man riding the horse up to the office with Cal and Matthew. He sat a horse like he was more comfortable in the saddle than he would be in an easy chair. She returned to her seat and looked up from her ledger as the men entered the office, her instant attraction to Evan's presence tilted her world on its axis. He was tall and muscular like Dad had been. His blue eyes danced when he looked at her too, but unlike Dad's amused adoration, Evan's held a heated passion that made Dylynn's cheeks flush. Her hand felt the heat of Evan's touch long after the introductory handshake ended, and it took every bit of control she had to keep herself composed while she took down Evan's information. Once she sent him back out to find Cal, she slumped into her desk chair completely out of breath from the effort. I found her still dazed in her chair a few minutes later. "Dylynn! Are you alright? What happened?" She smiled, stood up, drifted dreamily over to look out the window and stated, "Nothing's wrong and I'm going to marry that man." A bold statement like that was out of character for Dylynn, but she wasn't wrong.

CHAPTER 9

We moved into our new house on a Sunday afternoon with everyone's help. Dylynn brought a picnic of cold fried chicken, potato salad and peach turnovers, and we sat on blankets by the creek to eat after all the wagons were unloaded. I leaned back against Cal's chest wishing I hadn't eaten so much. My appetite was ridiculous lately. Cal commented on how much food I was putting away at mealtimes, but Hannah was keeping a low profile, so my secret was still safe. I couldn't wait for everyone to go home so we could be alone. I was bursting to tell Cal about Hannah.

A whoop came from the creek. All eyes were drawn to Evan as he lifted Dylynn off the ground and kissed her square on the mouth. Planting her back on her feet, they turned to us. Cheers and well wishes went around for them on their obvious betrothal, and the others began packing up for the ride back to town. We sat out on the porch enjoying our first night in our new place. I could hear the faint calming sound of water flowing over rocks that rose up to us from the creek and I nestled into Cal as he put his arm around me. "I could die a happy man tonight, Beth. Having this place with you here by my side is all I could ever want."

"I don't know, Cal," I mused. "I think I want a garden with a path to the front steps. Maybe a little gate to walk through. Will you build me a picket fence with a gate? How about a little arbor to grow some wisteria? It would be so welcoming." He leaned down and whispered "Whatever you want, Beth. It's yours."

Turning my face to him I said I was ready to get everything unpacked and settled so we were prepared for guests. He looked confused and asked when we had guests arriving because I hadn't mentioned it until now. I took his hand that was resting on his leg and guided it to my stomach. "Hannah is on her way to us and she'll be here in about four months." With a question in his eyes, he asked, "Who's Hannah? I don't recall you talking about a Hannah." I laid both hands on his as it covered my waistline and told him that Hannah is our daughter. As he took in the news, I watched understanding dawn on his face. His eyes lit up as he stood. He picked me up to carry me across the threshold of our home and took me directly to our bed.

The next morning, I cooked Cal a hearty breakfast before we left for the stockyards. After we ate, he leaned back to make room for me to sit in his lap. "Hannah, huh? How do you know it's a girl?" With a lift of my shoulder I said I named her as soon as I knew I was pregnant. "But, what if it's a boy? Should we choose a name just in case?" I shook my head no, kissed him on the forehead as I got up to clear the table and said, "No. It isn't a boy. There's no need."

Hannah joined us early on a Friday morning about four months later. Cal wanted to go to town for Mom and Dylynn, but I knew there wasn't time. She was ready and unwilling to wait for anyone else's help entering this world. Assuring him we could do this together, I explained what he needed to do. Within an hour, Hannah's wail was filling our home. As Cal handed her to me, the sun's first rays came through our bedroom window. Cal lay down beside me to gaze at our perfect little wonder, and my love for him welled up and fell from my eyes. "I love you, Cal. We've been given so many blessings in such a short time. I'm so overwhelmed, I don't have the words to thank God for it all. I feel sorry for people who never know this kind of love." Cal cleared his throat and hid his face in my neck. Choking through his emotion he said, "I do too, Beth. I didn't believe I could love you more today than I did yesterday, but seeing you hold Hannah is almost more than my heart can take. She will grow up knowing she came from a fire so strong her soul will carry our spark as long as she lives."

CHAPTER 10

Dylynn was a breathtaking bride. So much so that Evan had to stifle his gasp and choke back tears as she walked through the church door toward him. As Cal and I stood up for them with Hannah in Cal's arms, they committed their lives to each other in a small ceremony of our closest friends and family. The weather was beautiful for the outdoor reception. Evan and Dylynn invited the whole town, and we danced into the night until we wore out the band.

A few months later, on a Sunday afternoon, we all gathered at Mom's for supper. As Dylynn uncovered an apple pie for dessert, Evan leaned his chin on his folded hands and sighed. Dylynn kept serving the pie and said, "It's time, Evan. Just get started and it'll get easier once we have it out." Of course, this quieted us and all eyes were on Evan. "The government is concerned about the Sioux forming an uprising in South Dakota and I received conscription papers last week. I'm required to report to Fort Pierre by the end of next month." Evan dropped his head into his hands and couldn't say anymore. Mom rushed to him and held him saying, "I'm so sorry, Evan. I know how you feel about the government's interference in the Indians' lives. How long are they making you serve?" Shaking his head, he looked up at Mom to tell her they were asking for five years but that it could be longer depending on whether the government decided the situation was under control. Holding his face in her hands, Mom assured him that we'd pray for God's will to guide him until he could come back home to Dylynn. At this, Dylynn put down the plate she held and said, "I'm going with him. They're providing homes for some of the cavalry families in Fort Pierre and I want to be there so I can see Evan when he comes in for reports."

"No," mom said in a quiet demand. "It isn't safe there, Dylynn. We need you here to help with the stockyards and Evan can come home for visits when he's allowed leave." Dylynn grabbed Mom in a fierce hug, "Mom, I know this hurts. Evan and I have time to train replacements before we have to leave. With all the cowboys in town, we'll find someone to handle the horses who Evan and Cal can trust. Kelly Firsch has been helping me in the office since her husband passed and I can teach her to do my job. Besides, she could use the extra money to help with the kids since she's on her own." Mom bit her lip to stop the tears and stood there shaking her head in denial.

"I'm sorry, Mom. We don't want to go, but we aren't willing to be apart. I'm going with Evan and the decision is made. We aren't asking your permission. We're telling you we're going and what we'll do to help before we leave." Dylynn's respectful tone took the starch out of Mom's shoulders and she deflated onto her chair. Staring unseeingly at the floor, Mom sat there nodding to herself while the room fell silent. Drawing herself back to us, she straightened her posture and turned to Dylynn. "It's what I would've done. Hell couldn't have kept me from leaving Ben's side. You've been raised to understand a dedicated marriage. I would be wrong to ask you to stay."

Dylynn hugged me hard, climbed into the wagon and softly begged Evan, "Please, we have to go now." I watched them until they were over the hill. She never looked back and I couldn't keep my promise to be strong. As soon as Evan touched the reins to the horses' backs, my heart broke wide open. Had she turned back to wave she'd have seen me falling apart. Hannah cried in Cal's arms so I took her and cuddled her to me for comfort. Cal stood behind me until I started walking. "Where are you going, Beth?" I just shook my head and kept walking. I was going home. There would be no work for me today. I needed time to put my heart back together and get my head on straight before I mounted a horse to handle restless cattle.

CHAPTER 11

Grant passed that summer. We had horrible heat for days without rain. The drives were coming in slower now that barbed wire fences were restricting ranchers from crossing the plains. The railroads were making cattle transport easier. There weren't enough drives coming in to cover payroll so we had to lay off half of the stockyards hands. Grant was pitching in at the pens so Cal could work with the horses over at the corral. I was on the other side of the yard when I saw him stumble to the fence. Hanging onto the fence rails, he slid his hands down from one rail to another as he sagged. Thinking he'd fainted, I grabbed my canteen and ran to him. I had the top off and was tilting his head back to make him drink when I realized his eyes weren't looking back at me.

A month later, I went to check on Mom and let her play with

Hannah. Calling her name as I entered the house through the front door, I set Hannah down to go find her. She waddled to the back and came back alone. We walked to the kitchen window overlooking the backyard and I saw Mom sitting in her favorite spot. She and Dad had put the bench under the shade tree right after we moved in, and they spent most nights out there together after supper. They would sit quietly talking and laughing, always in the same position. Dad's arm would be across the back of the bench and Mom would be tucked into his side with her head on his shoulder.

I stood just outside the back door and watched her for a moment. Her head was down and she was a picture of stillness. I hated to interrupt her, certain she was either reliving a memory of Dad or praying. I moved quietly to the side of the bench hoping my presence wouldn't startle her. A teacup lay broken at her feet, and in her hand was her favorite picture of Dad but there were no tears of grief this morning. He must have met her as soon as she passed over. The trace of a grin still remained on her lips and her face was a portrait of perfect peace.

Word was sent to Dylynn. Evan was away on duty and it wasn't safe for her to travel back to Ogallala alone. She was devastated that she couldn't be here for the funeral and wrote in a letter that she and Evan would try to be home for Thanksgiving. I functioned in a muddled semi-awareness for the next two days as Cal helped me make arrangements for Mom's service. Staring at the dresses hanging in her closet, I saw nothing appropriately subdued enough for a burial dress. Mom loved color and it carried into her wardrobe. There were no drab funeral dresses here. Maybe I should look for something in town. Tapping my fingernail to my lips while I passed my hand over the swirling patterned fabrics of each dress, I decided to buck tradition. Mom wouldn't have wanted a somber burial dress. She's back with Dad. She'd want a party dress. Laughing to myself, I knew Mom was there with me guiding me to choose a dress that would knock Dad's socks off. A glimpse of emerald at the back of the wardrobe brought back a flood of memories.

There was a pie auction and dance in town shortly after we moved here. Work was all we'd done since we arrived, and we were thrilled to have an evening of fun in store. Dad took us to town and bought each of us a new dress just for the occasion. Of course, I wanted black, and Mom said I was gloomy as she pointed to a gorgeous navy blue cotton with sheer flowy cap sleeves. Mom knew I would fall in love with it as soon as I tried it on. I waited patiently with Dad while Mom and Dylynn looked at every dress in the store. After a half hour of trying on and discarding everything, Mom said she'd make do with something she had. Maybe she could rework one of her dresses with some new ribbon. She headed to the notions counter to find something she could update an old dress with, and Dad winked at me. Turning to the dressmaker, he nodded and came to sit by me with a sly grin he couldn't hide. "Watch this," he said with a chuckle. The seamstress waltzed out of the back room she'd retreated to after Dad's nod cradling a fall of shimmering emerald silk. "Excuse me, Mrs. Sandrick, but Mr. Sandrick asked me to make this dress for you a month ago when the new fabrics arrived from Omaha. He bought the whole bolt and chose the style from our fashion book." The ribbon in Mom's hands drifted back to the counter as they lifted involuntarily to her gaping mouth. "Ben! What did you spend?! This is just a pie auction, for goodness sake!" Dad leaned back in his chair and crossed his legs acting as if he was bored, "Try it on, Seline. If you don't care for it, Dylynn can wear it to the dance."

"She will not!" Mom shrieked and she nearly skipped to the dressing room. Mom glided out of their bedroom the night of the dance after she'd finished dressing and she was magnificent. The dress draped perfectly and fit as if she'd been sewn into it. The jewel-colored silk set off the jade flecks in her eyes and the look she and Dad shared when she walked out to the sitting room where we waited made Dylynn and I so uncomfortable we went out to the porch to wait until Grant and Cal joined us.

Cal's boots hitting the front steps of Mom's porch jolted me back to the present, and I was giggling when he walked in to find me holding Mom's emerald dress. "What do you have there, Beth?" Cal asked warily. He'd left me here to choose a burial dress and I'm sure he expected to find me staring at the wall helplessly when he returned, so my change of demeanor puzzled him. "And, why are you grinning like a schoolgirl about to play a trick on the teacher?" Holding up Mom's dress with one eyebrow cocked to rule out any rebuttal, I said, "This is the dress Mom's going out in and she wouldn't have wanted it any other way."

We placed her beside Dad in our family plot at the cemetery next to the church. Cal took a flower from the family spray as we left the burial and laid it on Grant's grave on our way out. It was up to Cal and me to make the stockyards work now. I prayed we wouldn't let them down.

CHAPTER 12

Cal and I took the money from the sale of Grant's ranch and Mom's house and bought a herd of yearlings to build up our stock at the corral. Our hope was to gain enough revenue from breaking and selling the horses to supplement the loss from the stockyards. Matthew was handling things at the stockyards. He and Kelly had developed a romance after being paired together in the office since Dylynn left and they had recently married. They worked well together and were so loyal to Cal and me. We couldn't have kept things going without them.

As we shifted our efforts to the horses, Cal and I spent most of our days at the corral. We had regular check-ins with Matthew and Kelly, and the four of us spent hours together over the winter months playing cards to pass the time. Kelly's kids loved to entertain Hannah and she found them amusing. They were friends who had become our family. Evan and Dylynn were faring in Fort Pierre, or I should say Dylynn was faring. Evan seldom got to come home since the discord between the Sioux and the government had heightened. We shared long letters to keep each other informed of our lives, but we hadn't seen each other since the day they left. There was a gaping hole in my heart that only Dylynn's presence could fill, but I learned to focus on my love for Cal and Hannah to get me through.

Hopefully, we could get through this winter and the horses we were working would sell in the Spring.

CHAPTER 13

The worst of winter was behind us. It was still cold, but the ice didn't have to be broken for the horses to drink from the water troughs anymore. Cal and I had a great herd ready to sell and we already had a deal in place for our next herd of yearlings after the current stock was sold. Hannah turned two and loved being at the corral with us, so Cal turned one of the stalls into a play area for her. We could put her in there and keep an eye on her while we worked the colts in the corral. She jabbered and sang nonstop while she played and watched us work. When she was quiet we'd peek in to find her curled up for a nap in the hay. She alerted us to her waking as soon as we heard her laughing and singing again. We joked that we better not have any more kids because they wouldn't be as easy as Hannah. She was happy wherever she was and made fast friends with anyone at the corral or stockyards. Her happy

"Hi!" attracted their attention and she was often found charming a buyer before we could come out of the corral to meet them. Cal had some tiny britches made for her that looked just like mine and she insisted on wearing boots like us. There was no sense making her spend her days in dresses when she was toddling around in the barn.

She was babbling to the colts in a neighboring stall one afternoon when I heard her say, "Hello, Mister! Who you?" I walked over to her play area and didn't see anyone. "Who are you talking to, Hannah?" She pointed to the back of the barn and said, "Man ova there, Momma." Starting to turn to the barn to make sure she was only imagining things, I heard Cal holler my name. My heart lurched at the sound of the hoof hitting Cal as the horse reared. Blood was running down Cal's face from his brow. Knocked on his back from the blow, he rolled to avoid being under the horse's next hoof fall. Pushing to a stand, Cal staggered to the fence to get his bearings. I'd reached him by then. There was a deep gash over his eye that would need stitches, but he seemed to be fine. He tied his bandana around his head to stop the blood flow. He was staring over my head at the barn behind me and I worried he might have a slight concussion. "Cal, look at me. I need to make sure you're alright." Snapping my fingers in his face to get his attention, I begged, "Cal, please be ok. Look at me."

Breaking out of his disbelief, he sprang into action, "Beth, the barn is on fire!" He hadn't been in a trance. His brain was trying to register why there was smoke coming from the back of the barn in his addled state. Turning to look, I felt Cal rush past me as he hollered, "Hannah can't get out of the stall and I have to get the herd out! Get Hannah and go get Matthew, Beth!" We bolted into the barn and the smoke was already so thick we couldn't see to the back where the flames were already licking up toward the hayloft. Hannah had crawled up the side of the stall and was reaching for me when I got to her. Tucking her to me, I headed for the office to get Matthew but he was already on a dead sprint toward me. He'd seen the smoke from the office window. Kelly was close behind him and held her arms out for Hannah when she reached me at the edge of the fence around the barn. I kept moving and yelled at Kelly to come with me. Clutching Hannah tightly, a movement in my peripheral made me turn to look between the office and the barn as I moved us away from the smoke. A burly man on a midnight black horse was riding away from the back of the stockyards at a hard gallop. Any other time my mind wouldn't have let it go, but everyone's safety and saving the horses was pressing in on any misgivings I had about the stranger.

At the steps of the office, I sat down with Hannah to inspect her for burns. Although she was crying in fear, she was unharmed. I handed her to Kelly, asked her to keep Hannah away from the barn and to go get help, and I rushed back to the barn to help Cal and Matthew free the herd. "God, please help us! If we lose this herd, we won't recover." It couldn't be. The loss of our parents, the slowing of the drives and now this. I just kept saying it in my head over and over, "Please, no, God. Please help us."

The smoke had drawn attention and men from town were starting to arrive to help. The corrals were cloaked in a choking, heavy haze that stung my eyes. I strained to look for Cal, but I couldn't tell which man was him. The panicked horses and the men trying to direct them to safety were ghostly movements in and out of the smoke as it rolled out of the barn from all sides now. Where was Cal?

Out of the chaos, I finally heard my name, but it wasn't Cal who was calling out to me. Matthew stumbled out of the black cloud with Cal's prone body thrown over his shoulder. Tears ran rivers through the soot on Matthew's face and he was coughing out a raspy, "Get help, Beth! Get help!" He fell to his knees and gently laid Cal down. "I found him knocked out near the back door of the barn. He'd gotten the door open and pushed most of the horses out of the back half of the stalls, but a rafter must have come down on him." Lying down beside Cal, I put my ear to his chest. I couldn't feel the rise and fall of his breathing and I couldn't hear his heartbeat through the roaring in my head. "Please, no. Come on, Cal! Come back to me. You can't leave us!" I moved behind him to rest his head in my lap and felt the blood and the brokenness at the back of his skull. After cradling his head on my leg, I took my hands away from his head and they were soaked with blood. Doc's bag landed beside me and Doc was there. He leaned his head down to Cal's chest and then to Cal's mouth and nose. Leaning back, he took my stained hands in his and shook his head from side to side. When I comprehended the finality in Doc's eyes as he dropped my hands to wrap his arms around me, my agony overtook me and the sob that tore through my body would haunt my dreams for the rest of my life.

My Cal. My beautiful strong man lay motionless beneath me as my tears fell on his face. How long we stayed like that, I couldn't tell you; me holding Cal, Doc holding me and Matthew stunned into silence beside us while he sat with his head in his hands.

CHAPTER 14

I refused to hold Cal's funeral in the church. It felt confining and lacked the freedom I thought Cal's soul needed. God was with us just as much if not more on the hill where I asked to have chairs set up for the service than He was inside the walls of that church building. I had been there too many times in the recent months saying goodbye to those I loved. Well-meaning friends offered to take Hannah so I could be alone to grieve, but I wouldn't allow her out of my sight. Kelly had been arranging the food people were bringing in the kitchen and came into the living room where I sat in Cal's chair with Hannah. "Hannah, would you like a cookie? Beth, let me take her outside for some air while you go lie down. I'll stay and watch Hannah while you rest a bit." I kept my gaze out the window to watch the hill as the pastor, Matthew and Doc were setting up the chairs for Cal's service, "No, she's fine.

We're fine. Thank you, but I need Hannah to stay right here with me." Kelly quietly moved back into the kitchen and left me to stare out the window, with Hannah safely tucked into my arms.

Rushed footsteps fell on the front porch and the door flew open as Dylynn burst in. She took in the quiet house and her eyes landed on my disheveled state. Kelly walked in to address the caller for me and ducked right back out at Dylynn's stern shake of her head. Dylynn turned to me, we locked eyes and I came apart. Swooping down on the footstool beside me, she didn't say a word. She laid her hand on mine where it rested on Hannah's back and she let me weep. Later, in my watch out the window, I counted four men setting up. Evan was here. He'd brought Dylynn to me because he knew I would need her. As I watched him solemnly go through the motions, I thought about what a good man he was. Cal would have done that for me, too. He would've left a war to get me to Dylynn. And then my sobbing started again and I cried myself to sleep in Cal's chair while Hannah dozed with me. Dylynn never left me. She just laid her head on my leg and kept her wordless watch over me.

She remained quietly beside me for a week, knowing when to let me ramble in my anguish over a life without Cal and running interference for me with all the townspeople who checked in on Hannah and me. The days ran together and I was unaware of a full week passing. The only tether holding me to this life was knowing Hannah needed me, or I was certain I would've crawled in that grave with Cal and they could have thrown dirt over us both. I made sure Hannah was fed and bathed. Dylynn gently took the brush out of my hand after I'd been mindlessly running it through Hannah's hair for half an hour. Through it all, Hannah was my rock. She didn't fuss, she ate what I prepared for her and she slept right beside me until I was ready to rise. Dylynn sat on the floor and put Hannah in front of her. As she braided Hannah's hair, she softly whispered, "It's time, Beth. I know you don't want to do this life without him, but you have to figure out how for Hannah. Evan's been going through the books with Matthew and Kelly. There are things that don't add up and I've been gone too long to know where to pinpoint the problems."

CHAPTER 15

Dylynn was right. The books didn't add up. There were entries for expenses I knew we didn't have and no receipts to prove the purchases. Matthew was hesitant and Kelly stared blankly at me when I asked them to explain. I hated to accuse Matt of anything after my history with him of jumping to conclusions, but his demeanor was off. He hadn't been the same since Cal died. I assumed the distance he'd been keeping from me was respect for my grieving and his own grief, too. This was different. This behavior felt cold and detached.

I watched the anger creep up his neck into a face flushed with rage. There was fire in his eyes when he lashed out, "I've watched Cal work these books and hide it from you for the last two years to support your horse dreams instead of investing in the updates we needed to stay competitive in the cattle industry. I'm not covering for him anymore and I'm sure not going to sit here while you blame it on me. I begged him to see how he was running the stockyards into the ground, but all he could think about was doing your bidding. Your idea to start breaking colts cost this business its success." Kelly ducked her head and wouldn't meet my eyes when I looked at her questioningly. Matt continued with spite and there was no mistaking the blaze in his eyes as it froze to ice, "I've accepted a ranch management position with a cattle baron in Colorado who will appreciate my experience and advice. I was going to stay until I knew you were on more solid ground, but your implication that I've stolen from you again is all I need to walk out the door now. I will arrange for our belongings to be shipped to us and I already have a buyer for our house. Kelly and I will be leaving tomorrow morning and you and your sister can figure out your own mess. I don't owe you people another moment of my life." With his parting words, Matt and Kelly hurried out of the office and left me sitting there speechless. These were Cal's and my dearest friends. We were family. How could they fool us all this time? By the time I wrestled through the betrayal and went to find them, they were long gone.

Cal? Fix our books? It wasn't possible. Cal was a good businessman and that kind of backhandedness wasn't in him. He was as ethical about business as he was honorable about his morals. I didn't question that he'd done it for a second. I knew from the guilty look in Kelly's eyes and the malice in Matt's biting words that they were both guilty of what Dylynn and I suspected. I was willing to hear Matt's side and help if there was truly a problem we could work through together, but I never dreamed he'd steal me blind. There was no saving things. Dylynn had gone over and over the numbers. Not only was I penniless, but I was deep in debt.

CHAPTER 16

Matthew and Kelly had loaded everything they were taking with them and were ready to light out before they met with Beth. They'd planned to run. Matthew did have a job at a ranch in Colorado, but it wasn't until they arrived there that Kelly found out it wasn't as the ranch manager. Matthew had glossed over the details once again. Kelly was so tired of his lies. She agreed that Cal and Beth didn't appreciate everything they contributed to the stockyards, and she felt they were entitled to the money they'd been siphoning. Whatever was going on with the man in Texas made her uneasy, and the burly man Matthew was meeting behind the office when the barn fire started made her skin crawl. When she questioned Matthew, he snorted and told her it was his business how he provided for them and to stay out of it. The threat in his eyes was enough to keep Kelly from asking again. He'd never raised a hand to her, but rage would come over him from time to time that generated a meanness Kelly feared.

The ride to Colorado was long and they stopped little. Only when the horses were on their last legs would Matthew pause for rest. By the time they reached the ranch where Matthew's new job awaited, Kelly was so worn down she was fighting a cold. She sat in the wagon shivering with fevered chills while Matthew spoke with the owner to get directions to the manager's quarters. Matthew slammed back into the wagon and angrily clucked the horses into movement. He stopped the wagon in front of a row of small cabins. Kelly dreaded the time this next meeting would take. She just wanted to get to their home and sleep, but this stop wasn't a meeting. Matthew jumped down out of the wagon seat and started unloading. "Matthew, why are you leaving our things here?" she asked. "This is it, Kelly. We're living here. Get down and go inside if you're sick. I'll take care of the unloading." Too sick to argue, Kelly climbed down and drug herself into the tiny cabin. Dropping onto the tick-striped mattress, she slept.

Light hit the backs of Kelly's eyes and she rolled over with a groan. Her body ached and she was on fire. Matthew was gone and their belongings sat stacked in a pile in the center of the cabin. She rose to get a drink, but there was no water. Grabbing a pail by the door, she trudged outside to find a pump. She was so parched and her skin felt prickly. Her eyes blurred as she took in her new surroundings. It was quiet. The barn sat off a ways and she didn't see Matthew's horse tied to any of the fences. He must already be out with the owner checking cattle. Pumping water into the pail took all her strength. The fever made her weak and depleted her of any energy. She returned to the one-room house, gulped some water and fell back into sleep. What felt like minutes was actually hours that had passed when Matthew shook her awake. "Is there nothing ready for supper? Kelly, I've been out all day and I come home to no food?" Peering at him through one squinted eye, she murmered, "I'm sick, Matthew. I barely made it to the pump and back for water." Matthew kicked the side of the bed and left the cabin in a huff.

CHAPTER 17

Days later, Kelly finally had the strength to get out of bed. Waking in the blanket she'd been wrapped in when they arrived, she found her traveling dress rumpled and odorous. After multiple trips to the pump for water, she boiled enough to fill the tub she'd dragged into a corner. For privacy, she hung a sheet from the ceiling in case anyone barged in while she was bathing. Feeling refreshed after cleaning herself up, she set to work on unpacking a few things for the kitchen to cook a meal. She was ravenous. Where had Matthew been while she was sick? It didn't look like he'd been here at all.

Later that evening, he stuck his head in the door and said, "Good, you're awake. I was hoping I wouldn't have to eat another meal of beans out of the cowboys' pot." Sitting down to eat the stew Kelly prepared earlier, he looked at the unpacked trunks and asked, "Are we going to unpack?" Kelly's confused look met his accusing one, "I thought maybe this was temporary until the manager's house was ready. I didn't want to unpack everything if we'd be going to the other house soon." Pushing back his plate, he dropped into the chair by the bed. "We're not moving to the manager's house. There is no ranch manager. The owner does his own managing. I'm a hand, Kelly. This is all there is." Kelly stammered, "But you said you'd accepted a management position. I don't understand." Matthew bellowed back at her, "I know what I said. Just leave it, Kelly. I get so sick of your questions. I told you this is it, so this is it." The next morning as he walked out the door, he looked back at Kelly and said, "Get us unpacked. I'll be back around dark."

This would be the first of many hired hand's homes Kelly would unpack and pack back up. She and Matthew moved around from ranch to ranch. He couldn't keep a job because the owners were always at fault for something. It was never Matthew to blame for his lack of staying employed. The moving and poor living conditions were proving difficult for Kelly, and her health was failing. The current house in Montana was drafty, and the fireplace barely kept the small home warm enough. Kelly woke in the night with fever and chills. She got out of bed, wrapped herself in a blanket and walked over to stoke the fire. A spell of dizziness hit her and she lost her balance. Matthew never heard the thud of Kelly's head hitting the stone ledge of the fireplace over his snores. He found her staring into nothingness when he woke the next morning.

CHAPTER 18

A buyer from the stockyards in Chicago purchased what remained of Sand-Rich Stockyards. What they planned to do with it, I had no idea. There was so much work to do to bring it back to what it once was. I had to walk away. There was nothing else I could do. The purchase amount was enough to cover the debts we owed, but very little was left for Hannah and me to live on afterward. Dylynn wanted me to move to South Dakota with them, but I wasn't ready to leave behind the home Cal had built for us.

After convincing Dylynn that Hannah and I would be alright for a few months on the remaining funds from selling out, she and Evan left us staring after them as they headed north out of town. I reached for Hannah's hand and plastered a brave smile on my face to assure her. Walking back into the house felt like crossing the threshold into a stranger's home. The beautiful things Cal and I collected had all been sold to gather as much money as possible and only the necessities stood with us in the lonely space. Hannah fell asleep, so I took out the paper to look for work.

It was slim pickings. My options were saloon girl or saloon maid. I'd already visited the bank and stores in town to ask if any help was needed, but no one had anything for me. Resting my head in my hands, I asked God to provide for us. My pride wasn't going to feed us when the last of the money ran out. I was going to have to sell our house and it devastated me to think of leaving the memories we'd made. Folding the paper, there was a small ad on the back page I'd missed. "Governess needed in Dalhart, TX. Mature woman preferred. $20 a month plus room and board. Telegraph T. Bauer" Twenty dollars a month?! That was a generous amount. Nevermind the room and board. I woke Hannah and went directly to the telegraph office to post notice of my interest to T. Bauer.

The next day, a response was waiting for me when I checked at the telegraph office. With an aching heart and a sigh of relief, it was confirmed that Hannah and I were leaving Ogallala. "Position yours, Ms. Richards. Train fare reimbursed on arrival. Expected in 2 weeks."

A visit to the bank to inquire about selling our home yielded a buyer on the spot. The banker's son was marrying soon and wanted the place as well as any furniture I could leave. The papers would be drawn up in time for me to sign before we needed to leave. Hannah and I walked home slowly while I thanked God for answering my prayers, and battled sobs with every step. My fear of not being able to take care of Hannah was alleviated, but I hated myself for leaving everything Cal and I had built. Fighting the sinking feeling in my gut and the stinging burn of the unshed tears took everything I could muster. I wouldn't let Hannah see my sadness. She needed light in her life. Looking up, I asked God to shine His light on us. Trudging up the stairs to the front porch, fixing supper, getting Hannah to bed and going through the evening motions were sheer acts of will. After Hannah was sleeping, I wandered outside and leaned on the gate. Burning acid rose at the back of my mouth as supper threatened to come back up and I went to my knees in the grass. I let the wracking sobs overtake me, and when there was nothing left I went back inside and began packing our things.

CHAPTER 19

Hannah was so good on the train ride. Rather than sulking in sadness after I told her we were starting over someplace new, she accepted it with an understanding years older than her age. In all the darkness I was swimming through since Cal's death, she was my only reason for hanging on. Without her, I could have easily succumbed to the selfish thoughts about joining Cal that haunted my heart.

The smoking black bulk of the train came to a stop. Out the window of our car was the town of Dalhart. The view from the other window was a flat expanse of bare land that went on into the horizon. Waves of heat shimmered in the distance and dust followed the people as they walked the streets of town. I was thirsty just looking out the window. I'd heard this land held a far different scape than what we were used to in Nebraska, but I had no idea it would feel so desolate. I caught Hannah's concerned look in her reflection on the window. With a deep breath and a little smile, I nudged her playfully. "The first thing we're doing is getting a lemonade from that nice lady on the platform. Whew! I could drink the whole pitcher, nevermind the cup. How about you?" She giggled and turned her attention to the platform to find the fastest route to the lemonade.

Stepping off the train with Hannah, I noticed a stern-faced man walking out of the crowd. "Ms. Richards?" When he stopped in front of me, my mind assessed him while we went through the polite introduction to each other. Menacing, my inner voice said, and immediately countered that with the reminder to stay positive. It was too soon to judge. After all, he was smiling just a bit and seemed courteous. I think I saw a spark of irritation when I straightened my posture to face him and he realized we were on eye level. For a burly man, he wasn't overly tall—more husky. When he reached for our suitcases, I noticed his hands were large and meaty. I missed Cal's hands; so strong and perfectly shaped. Inhaling the broken sigh I wanted to release, I squared my shoulders and asked Mr. Bauer if he'd mind me making a quick stop at the lemonade stand to treat Hannah. He gently chucked Hannah's chin and gave her a friendly wink. "Lemonade'll cool us right down. Let's get a cup and clear out of here."

Our bags were settled in the wagon and Mr. Bauer asked if

there was anything we'd be needing from town. Before we went to his ranch, he needed to stock up on supplies. Every trip to town had to be taken advantage of here because the ranch was two hours from Dalhart. "We have most of what we'll need, but there are a few items I'd like to purchase. Thank you for asking." He tipped his head and we struck out. "I'd like to introduce you to the shopkeepers and the banker. They'll need to know you can charge to the ranch accounts and it would help me if you could do some of the banking when you need to make trips to town." I responded with a nod and a smile as we wove our way through the midday bustle.

The people I was introduced to were kind, but I sensed a wariness from some of them. Mr. Bauer seemed to be respected. He was congenial, but there was no warmth in his exchanges with the shopkeepers. Our last stop was the bank. I needed to set up an account so Hannah and I sat down with a clerk to handle our business while Mr. Bauer went to the back office to visit with the banker, Mr. Sitton. When I finished with the clerk, Mr. Bauer waved me to the back. Hannah and I were introduced to Mr. Sitton, he inquired about my train ride and we went back out into the heat to load up for the drive home. We spent the time getting to know each other, and I had questions about what was expected of me other than taking care of Mr. Bauer's children since he'd mentioned me handling some of the banking.

There was only one child, a nine-year-old boy named Beau.

When I asked if there was any meaning behind the French name, Mr. Bauer shrugged. "His mother liked the name. I didn't care how she wanted to spell it. Before your next question lands about his mother, I'll just tell you she passed four years ago. That's all you need to know. I won't lead you into this blindly; I've struggled to keep help for Beau. You're the fourth woman I've hired in as many years. He's smart; too smart. Schooling bores him and it leaves his mind with too much time for mischief. I'm away from the house most of the day, so you'll have to figure out how to handle him. I plan to have him working more with me as he gets older, but I want him to be educated. I expect you to teach him what he needs on that side. I'll handle showing him how to be a man." Contemplating everything he'd just told me, and a lot that he purposely hadn't, I responded with the cool confidence I'd seen Dad use. "I appreciate you giving me the lay of the land. My parents insisted that my education come first when all I wanted to do was work the cattle with my dad, so I understand Beau's probably frustrated. I'll respect your boundaries on discipline, but he won't be allowed to run over me."

Surprise had Mr. Bauer looking at me. A hint of belittlement joined his tone, "Working cattle. I'm sure your father set you straight on that right away." Since I've had this conversation more than a few times, I answered without offense, "He sure did. He set me straight on my first horse and away we went." My face was smiling, but my eyes were serious. He half shook his head and raised his eyebrows, "You're welcome to ride the horses in your free time, but I have hands to help with the cattle. Your job will be to work with Beau and mind the house staff."

CHAPTER 20

The main house stood sentry behind a row of cedar elms that were intended to prevent road dust from drifting inside. The massive home was two full stories with dormers set into the steep roof that led me to believe there were bedrooms at the top rather than just attic space. Great, double doors served as the main entrance and sat back in the shade of a deep wraparound porch. The porch outline was carried out around the second floor as well to grant outdoor access to the second-floor rooms. Heavy wooden beams were the pillars bracing the porch and hanging pots of bright red geraniums splashed color that broke up the pale brick they called Texas blend. Shutters edged the windows in the same dark brown stained wood color as the beams and I was surprised by the warm welcome the house extended. I expected something more utilitarian and cold from Mr. Bauer, but maybe this was more of his wife's touch that she'd left behind.

We were ushered into the darkened front hall. Expanses of coffered wood walls ran the length of the hall and soared up to the vaulted ceiling in the great room. From this vantage point, I saw the second floor wrapped around the great room off three sides lending anyone up there clear sight of the chair and couches surrounding a towering fireplace made from the same brick as the exterior. The couches were leather the color of tobacco, and more splashes of red were tastefully added with pillows covered in a dense woven fabric that reminded me of horse blankets. A square rug nearly the size of the room stretched under the furnishings and carried the colors of the room in an appealing blend of reds, browns and yellows. On a quick inspection as we walked toward the staircase, I could see the home was spic and span. I imagined I could run a white-gloved finger over any of the surfaces and come up with no smudge on the glove. Mr. Bauer had mentioned he wanted me to mind the house staff, but I didn't see anything that looked one bit out of order. I wondered what minding was needed.

From the landing on the second floor, Hannah and I were shown to our rooms by a stiff woman who introduced herself as Bea. There was no smile as she gave us a tour of the home to familiarize ourselves with our new surroundings. She made curt introductions to others as we met them and moved through the home efficiently. We ended in the kitchen where a plate of warm cookies sat cooling on the counter. A kind lady who we learned was the cook, Marta, poured us each a cool glass of lemonade and invited us to sit down. We no sooner settled ourselves in our seats when the back door flew open and an angry boy I assumed was Beau came running in. Grabbing two cookies and whirling on his father who'd followed him in, Beau hissed, "I will not! You promised you were going to let me start working cattle with you and now you're making me spend the days in this house with the women. I'm smarter than every hand you have and you still won't let me quit school." Sneering in my direction, Beau said there was nothing I could teach him that he didn't already know. With that, he walked back out the door leaving all of us in an awkward silence. Before Mr. Bauer could ask me to excuse Beau's behavior, I held up a hand to stop him. Grinning, I winked at Hannah, looked Mr. Bauer in the eye and told him not to worry. Beau didn't know it yet, but I had his number. I was just like him at his age.

CHAPTER 21

"There's no rule that school has to take place indoors. Why don't you take me down to the barn and pens for a tour, Beau." Sluggishly, Beau stood from his seat in our little room designated for school at the front of the house, "Alright, but if Dad gets mad that you're out there, you'll be in trouble." I assured him we'd stay out of the way of the hands. As we walked out of the yard into the lane that went toward the barn, Beau kept his eyes on the cattle grazing in the pasture. Knowing I'd have to carry the conversation and because I had questions, I decided to test Beau's level of learning. "How many head does your dad run?" Beau looked at me with squinted eyes that were equal parts puzzled and intrigued, "We're at 90,000 right now because he just shipped." I nodded with impressed approval, "How many acres do you figure it takes to feed a herd that size?" He stifled a derisive snort, stopped and turned to me,

"I see what you're doing. You're quizzing me to see how much I know about ranching. All I want to do is help Dad run this operation. He thinks I'm too young and I don't know enough, but he doesn't talk to me enough to find out what I do know. I've paid attention.

"Dad came to Texas from Colorado after the war ended. He heard there were stray cattle wandering all over West Texas from the Spanish who'd been run out and the herds had been on their own so long they were overpopulating the state. He'd purchased 3,000 acres here and drove 2,000 head to this place when he started. It didn't take him long to realize he needed more acres per unit. He shipped half his herd the next Spring, took the profit and bought more land. He made one more gathering trip and brought back 4,000 head that time. Since then, he's been producing from his own stock, buying land and working harder on getting good bulls to get quality genetics. Dad's crossbreeds are hardy and don't have any problems surviving the drives. They bring top dollar and beef buyers are willing to pay it. This last shipment brought ten dollars a head. Do you know what scrap cattle bring? Maybe four or five bucks. This is why the rich people out east want Bauer beef."

As Beau educated me on the Bauer beef history, I watched his expression move from nonchalance into excitement. In the time it took for him to tell me his father's story, my heart opened to this boy who so badly wanted to be considered a man by his dad. It also broke. Beau clearly idolized his father and he was passionate about ranching.

We resumed our walk toward the pens and I followed Beau's gaze as it went back to the cattle. I wondered out loud, "How cattle can fatten from this dry grazing amazes me." Beau shot another glance in my direction, but this one held pity for my ignorance. With a hint of haughtiness, he informed me that cattle can process vegetation so well because they have four stomachs and anyone who knew beans about cattle knew that. Rather than correct him, I threw a question back. "Is it four stomachs or one stomach with four chambers?" Stymied, he climbed up on the bottom rung of the fence and hooked his arms on the top rung to turn his reddening face away from me. I joined him on the fence and detailed the four chambers of the ruminant digestive system. Surprisingly, he seemed to soak in the information rather than refute it. After a pause, he replied that the only animals more fascinating than cattle were horses. He followed with, "Are horses ruminants?" Shaking my head, I defined the monogastric digestive system and the four parts of a horse's large intestine. He was rapt and I realized animal science would be how I was going to keep Beau's attention. "Let's head back to the house and talk more about digestive systems. I'm hungry and I bet Marta has something ready for lunch." Beau dropped his chin in a curt nod, hopped down from his perch on the fence and met my stride as we strolled back to the house. From his look of concentration, I could tell questions were brewing. His curiosity was piqued,

"Ms. Richards, since horses are different, are cattle the only ruminant animals?" With a grin, I challenged him, "I'll tell you what. I'll give you half the answer. No, cattle aren't the only ruminants. Think you can guess the others?" He countered with a grunt and wanted me to just tell him. "Nope, your assignment for the afternoon is to find the answer in the library. We'll pick up on this in the morning. Please make a list of all the animals you find and bring the books you researched for the answers. After lunch, we're going to start on math." Beau's shoulders dropped and the boredom came back to his voice. "Math is dumb. When am I ever going to need math to be a cattle rancher?" On a laugh, I replied, "When your dad's last shipment of cattle brought ten dollars a head and he shipped 20,000, how much should his check from the sale have totaled?" A glimpse of the boy appeared in the grin spreading across Beau's face when he responded, "You can make math about cattle, too?"

CHAPTER 22

A year passed. Days sped by with Beau and Hannah. They'd forged a friendship after Hannah's relentless attempts to win Beau over and he'd quickly become protective of her. He liked to help her with her schoolwork and he kept close watch over her when they were around the hands and livestock. Hannah was laughing and a light danced in her eyes again. She was happy here and I loved Beau all the more for being such a big part of why she'd settled in so well.

Tyson (Mr. Bauer and I had dispensed with the formalities and now addressed each other by our first names) was impressed by Beau's improvement, and Hannah had captured his affections as well. I was grateful for a good job that challenged me and a beautiful place to raise Hannah. I tried to focus on the blessings and provision God gave us, but nights alone in my bed without Cal weren't getting any easier. My heart still ached and I dreaded the empty coldness of the bed I crawled into each evening. I used that time to talk to Cal as if he was still there beside me and I prayed God would give me the strength to keep living for Hannah. Were it not for her and the growing love I had for Beau, I would have had no fight against the temptation to do what was necessary to join Cal.

Tonight, I felt the darkness so heavily I feared it would suffocate me. I kept my spirits high for Hannah's sake and did not let her see my grief, but it wasn't hidden from Tyson. After dinner, we were all in the library. The children played a game that kept a steady stream of banter and laughter in the room. I held a book in my lap, but was lost in thought when Tyson interrupted my trance, "Beth, would you ever consider marrying again?" The question ripped through me so fiercely it took all I had to gather myself and answer, "My heart is still married to Cal. I don't believe I could commit myself to another and not feel as though I was being unfaithful. There are days I can hardly bear to think about how many years I will remain here before I see Cal again. Hannah is my light, and I'm so grateful to you for allowing the bond I have with Beau. Their love feeds my soul and helps me hang on." He leaned into the side of his wingback chair and looked up as his own grief took him inward. He exhaled and sighed, "It's the same for me. Her name was Shelly. To this day, I still love the sound of her name when I say it, but it's wrapped in so much pain that I don't use it around Beau or others for fear they'll see my weakness in how broken I am with her gone. I believe boys need a mother and girls need a father. I'd hoped someday I would be able to love again so Beau could have a mother, but I think that part of my heart is dead. I didn't expect you to last a month the day I brought you here. Beau's reactions to every caretaker I hired before you were abhorrent. It didn't matter how often I took the belt to him, he defied me more with each new hire. He ran them off before they were fully unpacked. You've made a difference. He respects you and it's clear he loves you. I don't know how to give him that. Hannah's easy. She wrapped me around her finger and I'm under her spell. Beau is different. He challenges me and pushes every button until I lose my patience." At this he paused and I took the opportunity to share my opinion. "He wants you to see him as a man. He challenges you because he wants you to respect him. He wants to be by your side in everything that is this ranch. He pushes your buttons because he wants your attention." Tyson studied me as I watched defensiveness spark in his eyes and then fade to agreement after considering my words. Following my opinion, I added some encouragement, "Beau's doing more than I ask with his schoolwork. He's exceptionally intelligent for a boy his age and more mature than most of your hands. I think he's an old soul. I find myself in conversations with him and have to remind myself that he isn't an adult. His wisdom about life far surpasses his age." Tyson's eyes shone with pride and he turned his head to watch Beau across the room. Then he shifted back to me, locked his eyes on mine and said it. "Beth, Beau needs you and I think I need you. I can't offer you love and I don't expect yours, but will you marry me? I want you and Hannah to stay." I felt my face blanch as instant nausea rolled violently through my stomach. With a quiet calm I didn't feel I looked at my hands resting in my lap and focused on the band on my left hand. "Tyson…I'm honored…I just…" Leaning forward, he rested his elbows on his knees and clasped his hands out in front of him as if he was going to pray. He bowed his head down so that neither of us were looking at each other and said, "You don't have to answer me right now. I thought you could come to love it here. With your ranching background, you're a perfect fit to help me run this place and raise Beau. At this point, I hate to separate you and Hannah from Beau and me. If there are terms you can bring to me that would make marriage to me work for you, think them over. When you're ready to talk to me, we'll sit down and iron it out." With that, he retired to his room for the evening.

Safely back in my room, I lay awake listening to the night noises a still house makes while my heart shattered into more pieces than it was already. "Cal, I can't do this to you. God, please don't ask this of me."

CHAPTER 23

Opening my eyes would be admitting a new day had dawned, and I didn't want to face it. When I finally gave in and lifted my lids, I knew I'd overslept by the amount of light in the room. Bounding out of bed to dress quickly, I caught a glimpse out the window of Beau and Hannah in the side yard. Hannah's delight at being pushed on the tree swing was filling the yard with repeated demands that Beau push her higher. Her loud squeals had Beau joining in and both children were whooping with magical joy. I stepped out onto the porch outside my bedroom and watched them. The morning sun was bright and its beams were shining through the tree above them. One strong shaft held them in perfect light and the picture of them was more than my heart could take. Tears streamed down my face as I watched them play and I knew we had to stay. I couldn't take this from Hannah. I tore my eyes away from them and looked out toward the pens. Tyson stood on the other side of the fence, entranced by the same scene. Our eyes met, I saw the question in them and I surrendered. With a solemn nod, I sealed Hannah's and my future at Bauer ranch.

That evening, after the children were in bed, Tyson and I decided how we would proceed. Tyson was respectful of my request to keep wearing Cal's ring, and I agreed to an additional band that would accompany it as long as it wasn't ostentatious. We would keep our separate bedrooms and try to grow this celibate relationship as a friendship and partnership.

CHAPTER 24

I bristled every time the hands or house staff greeted me as Mrs. Bauer. Each utterance felt like a betrayal of my love for Cal. In my mind and heart, I would only ever be Mrs. Cal Richards. Over time, I hardened to it and it didn't grate on me as badly as it did in the beginning. Beau and Hannah were growing. Beau was so smart, he didn't need as much time with me to complete his learning. Thankfully, he was doing most of his studying on his own because he was about to surpass my knowledge. He went through books about animals so quickly we could hardly get new ones delivered in time to keep up with his requests. Proving his gift with animal husbandry, he was handling a lot of the doctoring for the cattle and horses. Often, the hands would ask him when they didn't know what was wrong and Beau would have the answer. If he didn't, he would read and research until he found it.

Hannah was a bundle of ceaseless energy. She loved riding and took any opportunity available to be on a horse. Tyson bought me a few colts to break now that I had more free time and Hannah was just as enraptured with horses as I was. She was a quick study and spent as much time as I did working colts and riding. Tyson had broken down and realized I was resourceful with the cattle, so Hannah and I got to pitch in when we wanted. She was my miniature reflection in almost every way. She had my love of horses and ranching, the blond plait running down her back was just like mine, but her eyes—those were Cal's. I swore sometimes he was looking at me through her eyes. I hoped he was proud of me.

Tyson and I had a routine of sitting down with the post each evening to catch up on correspondence. This was when we discussed our day, any business there was at hand or anything we needed to talk about that concerned the children. I had a letter from Dylynn! We corresponded as much as we could, but time between letters was always too long for me. I began reading it with a smile and dropped my coffee cup in shock. Tyson jumped at the noise and came to me, "What is it, Beth? What's wrong?" I just handed him the letter and fell back in my chair. Why, God? Why both of us? Evan was gone. Several of the men in his regimen had intercepted disease-laced blankets intended for the Indians. By the time they realized the blankets were infectious, it was too late. Evan died of smallpox and Dylynn had nowhere to go.

CHAPTER 25

Tyson and I arranged travel for Dylynn to come to the ranch and she arrived a month after I received her letter. She was a wisp of a woman when I ran out to meet her at the front gate. There were no tears when I wrapped my arms around her. In fact, she stood in place and didn't return my embrace. When I stepped back to look at her, her eyes were empty. She was a shell of my sister and I imagined this must have been what she had to deal with when I lost Cal. Tyson and I silently started walking toward the house with her and she just collapsed. Tyson caught her up in his arms and carried her to the guest room we'd prepared for her. After settling her on the bed, he left us alone and went back to the cattle. I did what she'd done for me; I sat with her and I didn't leave her side.

Two days after Dylynn arrived, she was still sleeping. I'd roused her a few times to get a few bites of eggs and toast down her. She drank a little orange juice and a few sips of water, but she refused more. I sat in a rocker beside her bed and held her hand. Hannah came in and asked if she was sick. I told her no, so she wanted to know what was wrong. "Come sit beside me, Hannah. Aunt Dylynn's broken, honey." Settling on the floor beside me, she looked up and asked, "Will she mend?" I took a moment to decide how I wanted to respond and chose honesty. Shaking my head, I said, "No, she won't. She will get stronger as the days go by and she'll learn how to live in her brokenness." Hannah contemplated that for a while and then stood to hug me. "You did it, Mom. Aunt Dylynn will too." And, my heart that I'd put back together so many times broke again at Hannah's words. Hannah slipped out of the room, I put my head down on the bed beside Dylynn and cried all the tears for her that she could not.

CHAPTER 26

Another year passed. Dylynn moved through her grief in waves. There were days she took long walks and came back late in the afternoon. She'd eat a snack Marta would prepare for her and sit in the kitchen while she ate. Marta's steady movement around the kitchen comforted her and they struck up a friendship. Between Marta and me, we shielded Dylynn from the others in the house so she could have her space while she relearned how to do life as just Dylynn.

Somewhere in all that time in the kitchen, Dylynn started pitching in with Marta and it became the way things were. Tyson was happy to let her stay there as we were all benefitting from Marta's and Dylynn's blended culinary gifts. They experimented with food from different cultures to broaden our palettes. We started having one evening a week that was designated to a certain country, and we all agreed Italy night was our favorite. We sat down to a table with a large rectangular pan in the center, crusty loaves of bread dripping with garlic butter, a fresh salad made from lettuce out of Marta's garden that had a bold, oily dressing, and we ate until we were stuffed. They called the entrée in the big pan lasagna. We learned that pasta is a staple in Italian food. It comes in many different shapes and sizes, but it's all mostly made of flour, water and eggs. Lasagna pasta, or noodles, is a thin sheet of pasta that's cut into three strips. Each strip is about three inches wide. They mixed browned beef with tomatoes, garlic, onions and oregano, and let it simmer for hours until the whole house smelled wonderful. To create the lasagna, they layered the pasta sheets, clotted cheese, the browned beef and tomato sauce and cheese. Then, it baked until everything was a bubbling, cheesy masterpiece. After we'd gorged on this new recipe, they brought out another pan. This was dessert and it was layered too. They had to pronounce lasagna and tiramisu a few times before we were all saying it correctly. What a wonderful night! Beau and Hannah had done a report for us that covered a quick history of Italy. Beau found a book in the library about European cultures. His ability to take research and make it into an interesting table discussion made Tyson and me so proud. He was a scholar and a cowboy, and he was turning into such a handsome young man. I was overcome with love for him and Hannah as I watched them entertain us through the meal.

After so much darkness for Dylynn and me, it was healing

to have the light of Beau and Hannah in our lives. Dylynn doted on them and spoiled them, and they returned her love with their own devotion. Tyson and I started teasingly rolling our eyes at each other secretly when the kids would prattle on about Aunt Dylynn. She was becoming the animated Dylynn I remembered and I was so grateful to have her here with us.

CHAPTER 27

Tyson's accountant passed away, and he had a chore getting the ranch books in order. I told him Dylynn handled the books for us at the stockyards and he gladly brought her in to help. After some precursory questions for Tyson, Dylynn dug into the books. Within a week, she had everything organized and accounted for. She worked with Tyson and me to implement a system that was more efficient and easier for all three of us to understand. Tyson could ask her a question at any offhand moment and she knew the answer or could go right to where the answer was in the ledgers. They worked well together when Tyson had to be in the office and I was thrilled that Dylynn had found some purpose. She was in her element here on the ranch. When she didn't have any bookkeeping to do, she was in the kitchen with Marta or helping me with the kids' schooling.

Beau was spending his days with Tyson and asked to stay with the hands to work if Tyson had other work to do. Hannah stayed with me most days. We'd get through her assignments in the mornings and work colts or ride in the afternoons until it was time for dinner. Evenings were spent in the library playing board games or charades, and the dark, quiet house I'd entered years ago was a distant memory. This house was now a home filled with love and laughter. The days were so good, but nights were the same routine. I'd settle under the covers and talk to Cal about my day. I seldom fell asleep without the heaviness in my heart that had become my bedtime companion.

CHAPTER 28

At breakfast one morning, Marta was in the kitchen alone. I asked where Dylynn was and Marta said she hadn't been down yet. At this hour? Dylynn was usually up and around before all of us. She had never required much sleep so she'd always been an early riser. Thinking little of it, Hannah and I went outside to help the hands start separating the pairs. It was going to be noisy around here for a while. It was time to wean the calves and we all dreaded the bawling we were going to have to put up with for the next few weeks.

The next morning when there was no Dylynn in the kitchen, I was concerned. I went to her room and found her sitting on the side of her bed, face as white as a sheet. "Dylynn, what's wrong? Are you sick?" She nodded, "I must have caught a bug. I didn't feel well yesterday either. I'm nauseous and I just don't have any energy." I told her to get back in bed and went down to get her some tea and toast. I sat with her in her room while she nibbled the toast and finished her tea. Her color looked better and she said she felt better, but I thought she should rest. She snuggled back in and said she might see if she could sleep a little more. When we all got back in the house that evening, she was in the kitchen with Marta and said she was feeling much better. Beau and Hannah wanted to play a round of charades after dinner, so we all made our way to the library. It was Dylynn's turn, she stood up in front of us to act out her charade and suddenly ran out to the porch with an alarmed look on her face. I raced after her and found her throwing up in the bushes off the porch. She leaned back against the porch rail and said, "I don't know what's wrong. I took a nap this morning and felt great after I woke up. I've been going all day and it just hit me out of nowhere." I patted her on the back and put my arm around her waist, "Why don't you go on up to bed? I'll tell everyone you aren't feeling well. Maybe this will pass and it'll be over tomorrow."

But it wasn't. Dylynn was pregnant and I'd recognized the symptoms because I had experienced the same when I discovered Hannah was on the way. I had to hide my sudden onsets of sickness from Cal so he wouldn't figure out I was pregnant, and I never knew when the bouts of nausea would strike. I knocked on Dylynn's door the next morning and heard her chipper voice, "Come in!" She was dressed and ready to go help Marta with breakfast. I asked her how she was feeling and she said she was great, so we went down to the kitchen together. Marta was frying bacon and the smells met us on the back stairs before we made it to the kitchen. Dylynn stopped suddenly and ran back up to her room. I heard her bedroom door close and the soft wretching sounds. I fixed a tray of tea and toast and went back to Dylynn's room. "Dylynn? Can I come in? I brought you some toast." Her muffled yes came through the door and she was lying face down on the bed when I came in. "Dylynn, you don't have to keep anything from me. Do you know why you're sick?" She erupted into wracking sobs and cried, "I'm so sorry, Beth. How can you ever forgive me?"

CHAPTER 29

"How could you? Of all the disgraceful things a man could do, I never would have dreamed you were capable of this," I hissed in a whisper to Tyson. I found him in the weaning pen with the calves. I doubted Beau and the hands would hear us over the bleating calves, but I didn't want to take any chances. Tyson hung his head and walked away from the pen toward the open pasture. With steel in my veins, I followed on his heels. "You aren't going to walk away from this, Tyson, and don't you dare walk away from me. Turn around, look me in the eye and admit you took advantage of my sister in the worst possible way." When he stood there keeping his back to me, I walked around to face him and the toe of my boot bumped his. I let every bit of the chill in my blood freeze the ice in my stare as I stood in front of him challenging him.

THE LIGHT SEARCHER

He walked over to a rock jutting out of the field and sat down on it. Taking off his hat, he ran his hands through his hair and hung his head as he leaned over his legs. "I didn't take advantage of her. We've been working in the office together and something has happened between us. We lost control one time and it never happened again. I wanted to confess to you, but I didn't want to bring it to you without Dylnn's permission. I'm a coward, Beth. I didn't have the guts to handle this the way I should have." I couldn't process this. I couldn't make my mind work to move to my next thought. I was mentally and physically frozen in shock. Not so much the betrayal because Tyson and I had an arrangement, but how did he dupe me into thinking he was a decent man? I didn't really feel cheated on, but poor Dylynn. Single women who turn up pregnant have no prospects in this world. What was she going to do?

I walked to the barn, saddled my horse and rode. I didn't have a direction in mind. I didn't know where I was going. I just rode until I realized I was a long way from the barn. I found myself on a ridge that overlooked a windmill. It was beautiful here. From the ridge, I could see land until it met with the sky. There were wildflowers scattered around the catching tank under the windmill's pump. It was so still here, I couldn't hear anything but my own breathing. I sat on that ridge talking to Cal until I felt like I had my mind in a decent enough place to walk back into that house, and then I rode back to the ranch.

CHAPTER 30

The kitchen had been cleared by the time I made it back to the ranch, and there was a covered plate left on the table. I assumed Marta had left it for me, but I wasn't hungry. The house was still and the library lamps had been turned down. There was a light in the hall coming from the office so I headed there. Tyson and Dylynn were seated in the club chairs across from each other—both looking distraught. I crossed my arms in front of my chest, leaned against the door frame and waited for one of them to have the nerve to start talking. Tyson came to me, ushered me into the office and closed the door. "We've been waiting for you to get back. While you were gone, we made a plan for Dylynn.

"Victor is setting up the place in Colorado to get things going up there. I'm going to offer him a permanent position as ranch manager there if he will marry Dylynn and raise this child as his own. They will never need for anything and the child will inherit the Colorado ranch when they are of age to take over."

Dumbfounded, I looked at Dylynn. "And, you're fine with this. You're just going to move to the mountains with a man you hardly know and sweep all this under the rug like it never happened? Have you thought about what kind of life you're giving Victor?" Reeling on Tyson, I blasted him with, "What's he supposed to do, Tyson? Tell you no? What if he doesn't want this? You're putting him in a terrible position." Dylynn cleared her throat and asked me to sit down. "Beth, I don't expect you to forgive this. I'm ashamed to have to sit here and work this out with you two after everything you've done for me. Please hear me out. Victor and I are good friends and I trust him. He has been so supportive ever since I got here and walked with me a lot of nights so I wouldn't be out alone. There were entire walks that we didn't speak. He's never been anything but kind to me. I won't be moving with a man I hardly know, and I've already talked to him. I've known he would be leaving for Colorado for a long time since I started helping with the books. I've been working on getting everything set up for the Colorado operation, so it makes sense for me to go. I can handle the books for everything there and I'll be with someone I dearly love who will care for this child. Victor isn't accepting this proposal under pressure. He's doing it to chivalrously save my reputation because he treasures me as a friend. It's still early enough that no one will think the child isn't his if we get married before we leave. I'm begging you to agree to this."

I looked back and forth at the two of them sitting there waiting for my permission like it was my power to give it and laughed. With contempt I turned to Tyson, "This ties things up in a nice little package for you, doesn't it? You escape the consequences of your poor behavior and Dylynn and Victor take care of your mess for the rest of their lives. It's just a business transaction for you? You throw money at them and they're willing to hide your dirty secret? Tyson, you have been my best friend for years. I am devastated, and the sight of you disgusts me. How do I stay here knowing all this? What are we going to tell Beau and Hannah? That this child is their cousin? Tyson, this child will be Beau's sibling! Are you never going to tell him? What if it looks like you? What if Beau figures it out?"

Tyson finally found his voice and he rounded on me, "What do you want me to do, Beth? Sit them down and tell them the truth? How does that play out? I don't like the lie either, but is it right to drag Beau and Hannah into this? They need to be protected from this. We have to protect them from this." I countered, "You aren't protecting anyone but yourself. Don't pretend this is protection of Beau and Hannah. You two want to cover this up and make me party to it? I cannot believe you're asking that of me!"

Dylynn sighed, "What choice do we have, Beth? This is the best decision for not just Tyson and me, but for all of us. I want the kids to grow up with this child as cousins. What difference does it make if Beau never knows it's his sibling? They will seldom see each other. Please just say you'll agree to keep this between the three of us."

I left the office without saying another word and went to my room. I needed to talk to Cal.

CHAPTER 31

Tossing and turning didn't help. Talking to Cal didn't give me any clarity. I turned on my lamp, grabbed my Bible and let it fall open in hopes God would give me the answers. It opened to the book of Matthew, chapter six. Verses 14 and 15 say, "For if you forgive other people when they sin against you, your heavenly Father will also forgive you. But if you do not forgive others their sins, your Father will not forgive your sins."

My sins, God? You're going to talk to me about my sins at a time like this? I closed my Bible and set it back on my nightstand. Well, Cal? Anything to add? God just wants to lecture me about my sins right now. Tossing off the covers, I got out of bed and headed downstairs to the kitchen. I guess I was hungry after all. I ate everything on the plate Marta left for me and stared out the kitchen window blindly for I don't know how long. It dawned on me there was a light on in the bunkhouse. I went out to the mudroom and put on a coat and boots. Creeping up to the bunkhouse so I wouldn't startle the animals, I peeked in the window with the light on. It was Victor's room. His Bible was open on his bed and he was kneeling on the floor beside it with his hands folded in prayer. His eyes were closed and his lips were moving with the silent words he was speaking to God. I stood there knowing I should give him his privacy, but I couldn't walk away. I almost turned to go but I watched a few moments more, and then Victor opened his eyes. He was looking right at me. With the most peaceful look of acceptance, he held my gaze and nodded one time. I trudged back to the house, toed out of my boots, hung my coat and climbed the stairs to my room. I got under the covers, closed my eyes and had the clearest vision of Cal staring at me with peaceful acceptance and nodding one time. God, help me with this unforgiveness. God, please help me.

CHAPTER 32

The months turned into another year and a letter arrived from Colorado. The penmanship was Dylynn's. I missed her so much, but I was still so conflicted about keeping the true identity of this child from everyone. I took the letter to my room to read it alone.

My Dearest Beth,

I carried our baby boy full term and had a healthy delivery. He is beautiful and perfect, and Victor and I love him beyond comparison. We named him Benjamin Victor. I pray that you will love him as much as we do when the day comes that you get to meet him. He is almost three months old now and we are blessed by the joy he brings us. God is so good to us.

The ranch is doing well and we'll be ready for the next herd of cattle com-

ing up from Texas. Victor works long days to make sure everything is up to his standards and I'm so grateful to have a wonderful man who is my husband and friend. I never thought I could love again after Evan. Though I will always carry Evan in my heart, my love for Victor overwhelms me. We are truly happy and I hope that brings you peace.

Beth, I love you. I need you. Please write back. Please love us. All of us.

Your Sister,
Dylynn

I tucked Dylynn's letter into my Bible and went to the barn. I rode out to my spot on the ridge and watched the windmill turn, and I cried. All of this anger, resentment and rage just poured out of me. "Please love us. All of us." I do love you, Dylynn. All of you. I rode back to the ranch cleansed of the darkness that I'd carried with me for the last year. I asked Beau to get a wagon ready to go to town and then come inside. When he walked through the back door, Hannah and I were ready to leave and I had overnight bags packed for each of us. "What are we doing?" Beau asked. I smiled from my heart for the first time in a long time and said, "We're going to town to put together a nice gift for your new cousin. Victor and Dylynn had a baby boy and we're going to show him how much he's loved. After we get the gift bought and packed to ship, we're going to stay at the hotel and eat a fancy dinner to celebrate my new nephew."

CHAPTER 33

Tyson and I kept our business arrangement and that was all. Our friendship was over. I didn't see him the same after Dylynn left and I never recovered. We kept things cordial so the children weren't affected, but we gave each other a wide berth for the most part. One day, he walked into the office to let me know he'd hired a new ranch manager to run things here since he was going to be back and forth to the ranch in Colorado. Now that the cattle had shipped, Tyson was visiting Victor for weeks at a time to make sure Victor had it in hand. I assumed there was another reason for the visits, but never questioned his reasons. I would accompany him occasionally to spend time with Dylynn and the baby, but I preferred staying here. I agreed the manager was necessary and Tyson said he would arrive at the end of the week. I worked with the staff to make sure the guest house was prepared for the new manager and thought nothing of it when Tyson told me his name was Matthew. That Friday, Beau came in from the barn to get me and said Matthew had arrived. I went out with Beau and saw Tyson talking to the man near the barn. Something about his stance was familiar. He turned when Beau and I got to them and I stared at the man I'd hoped to never see again, Matthew Bishop. The years had not been kind to him since that last day he and Kelly left Ogallala, but I don't imagine anyone with a nature as mean as Matthew's would fare well. The nastiness has to be a poison that taints the blood.

Tyson began to introduce me and I interrupted him, "No introductions are necessary, Tyson. Mr. Bishop and I have met." Missing my venom, Tyson kept on, "I've known Matthew for years and he's going to be just what we need to keep things on track here while I'm on trips to Colorado." I smiled coldly at Tyson and replied, "References aren't necessary either, Tyson. Matthew's reputation precedes him. I know all I need to know." Turning on my heel I marched back to the house with nothing more to say.

That night Tyson railed at me for my rudeness and warned me that it would be in my best interest to adjust my attitude because Matthew Bishop wasn't going anywhere. I fought back with, "You've made me your partner in this operation and now you're going to tell me I have no say in who our ranch manager is? Much less, you're comfortable leaving Hannah and me here with a man I'm telling you we cannot trust?" He sneered at me as he went to the base of the stairs. Grabbing the newel post, he looked back at me with complete disregard and said, "I made you a partner and I can make you not a partner. That's up to you. Matthew stays. If you don't like it, you aren't obligated to stay." Where on earth would I go? I couldn't take Hannah away from this place she loved and I couldn't leave Beau. I resigned myself to the idea of being in such close proximity to Matthew Bishop and silently vowed that I would do everything in my power to protect Hannah and Beau from him.

CHAPTER 34

Tyson was aging. The trips to Colorado were taking their toll and he wasn't the strong, able-bodied man he was just a few years ago. I believed his decline had more to do with guilt eating him away, but those were his consequences to bear. We maintained our front for Beau and Hannah. They weren't blind. I knew they could detect the change in our relationship, but neither of them questioned us about it.

Beau was thriving. He was managing the ranch for all intents and purposes while Matthew lazed about. I avoided the man and Beau did too. He wasn't respected or liked by the hands, but Tyson kept him on. I suspected there was more to the working relationship. I watched and waited for something to be revealed to me, but nothing had surfaced yet. Matthew Bishop's day was coming. I felt it in every fiber of my being.

Hannah had gone from a coltish girl to a beautiful young woman. She was dearly loved by everyone and cherished ranching. When she wasn't working by Beau's side, she kept a steady stream of colts going in her spare time. She was a natural with horses. Her gentle way with them was a talent she developed on her own. I taught her everything I knew, but she had her own methods to develop trust with the animals. It was a wonder to watch her take them from the round pen to riding. Her fearlessness set me on edge, but I refused to inhibit her with my worry. I thanked God for her and the light she was to us all.

A man walked on the place one day looking for work and Beau hired him on the spot. Josh Tanner's parents were taken from him by a flash flood in the mountain area where they lived. He had no other family and wanted a fresh start. He fell in with the other hands quickly, was handy with a rope, good in the saddle and great with cattle. Although Beau never gave him a title, it was clear that Josh established leadership of the men and reported to Beau. Matthew couldn't stand him and tried to sabotage him several times, but the men always backed him. Finally, Matthew crawled back under his rock and left things alone when he realized he couldn't rid the ranch of Josh.

I hurried into the tack room one day looking for a lead rope and barged in on a private moment between Josh and Hannah. I was so taken aback that I hadn't realized they were together. I could read Hannah like a book and I only had to look in her eyes to see into her head. How this escaped me struck me right in the heart. Leaving the tack room, I got on my horse and headed to the ridge. I needed time with Cal. Settling into my spot with the view, I started pouring it all out to Cal. Did I disapprove of Josh and Hannah? No, Hannah was old enough to make her own decisions and Josh was a good man. The warning rattle jarred me from my thoughts. Sunning on the rock five feet from me was the biggest rattler I'd ever seen, and my rifle was on my horse too far for me to reach without startling the snake. I stayed frozen as I watched the snake coil, fearing any movement would prompt a strike. After what felt like an eternity, the diamondback slithered into a crevice and was out of sight. I slowly rose from the ridge, mounted my horse and headed for home. The trees were starting to turn with the cooler fall weather we'd been having and a breeze blew some leaves across my path. The autumn colors were a swirling kaleidoscope as they floated down in front of me and it occurred to me that letting go could be beautiful. Thank you, God. Thank you for that sign you just gave me. It's time to let my baby go. That was the core of my emotions—the evolution of time passing and the acceptance of my daughter's passage into the next chapter of her story. I just wish I didn't have to let go by myself, Cal. You should be here to hold me through this. As the thought went through my head, the sun came out from behind a cloud and shone warm on my back. I looked up into the clouds just as the sun ducked back behind another cottony puff. Drawing in a deep breath and releasing it on a sigh, I pointed my horse's nose toward the ranch and gave him the reins. I could hear Cal say, "It's time to give her wings, Beth."

CHAPTER 35

Spring came in like a lion with violent storms. The pens around the barn were so saturated with all the rain that the mud was as deep as our boot tops. During dinner one night, the strangest noise started working up outside. In puzzlement, we looked at each other and Beau hollered, "It's a tornado!" We rushed out to the porch and watched the cyclone cross the pasture less than a mile from the barn. It came down out of the boiling storm clouds and danced across the pasture, kicking up thick walls of dust and brush each time it met the ground. In fascination, I stood and watched the devilish cone until it pulled back up into the sky and was gone.

Resuming our dinner, Hannah pointed out that we probably should have gone to the root cellar instead of standing on the porch. Beau joked, "Ha! They'd have found us all dead under the porch ceiling with shocked expressions and slack jaws." The picture of it had us all in hysterics. Every time the laughter settled down, Beau would make a wide-eyed, open-mouthed face at Hannah and we'd start up all over again. God, I love these kids. Thank you for the light that they are in my life.

Later, in the library, Hannah sat beside me and laid her left hand on my leg. A thin band of gold, inlaid with a row of rectangular diamonds, was on her ring finger. I pulled her to me and whispered, "Yes, honey. He's the one." Letting go with one arm so I could invite Josh in for a hug, I said out loud, "We have a wedding to plan!" Hannah beamed at Josh and Josh looked at her like there was no one else in the room. I remember Cal looking at me the same way and I was so thankful Hannah would know real love. Hannah didn't want a big wedding, "Just something private here on the ranch, Mom. Just us and the hands are all we want. Maybe Uncle Victor, Aunt Dylynn and Ben could come for a visit so they can be here too?" I kissed her temple and agreed, "Of course, anything you want. When do you want to have the wedding?" Hannah looked at Josh and he nodded, "I don't care. I'll marry you tonight, right here in this room, but anytime is fine with me. What do you think?" Hannah went dreamy-eyed and said she'd always pictured a fall wedding on the front steps of the house.

CHAPTER 36

I sent a letter to Tyson with Hannah and Josh's news and asked him to have Victor, Dylynn and Ben plan a visit the first part of October for the wedding. The house buzzed over the next several months with preparation for the summer shipment of cattle and a wedding. Hannah ordered a bolt of cream silk jacquard and spent evenings after dinner behind a closed door with Marta while they created her wedding dress. I stood at the door to listen for any clue as to the secrecy, but neither of them would tell me what they were doing. There were mischievous looks between them anytime the dress was mentioned and I caught Hannah winking at Marta one time when I asked how they were progressing with the dress. What were they up to?

Along with her silk, she ordered a matching jacquard for me in a dark, rusty salmon color that was so rich. She didn't tell me her color choices until she brought the fabric out of the crate of goods she'd had shipped. "You look amazing in fall colors, Mom. I don't care what your dress looks like. Make anything you want. I just want you to wear something made from this fabric." My Hannah. It's her wedding and she chose her colors based on what she knew I loved. Leave it to her to be so thoughtful. "Hannah, I would have worn pink if you'd wanted it." Hannah scowled, "Pink? Mom! You and I don't do pink. We aren't those women." And we both laughed.

I knew exactly what I wanted to do with my fabric, but I was going to wait until Dylynn got here. She was much better at sewing than me and she would know how to make my idea come alive.

The cattle gathering went smoothly and we got them shipped before Tyson made it back from his latest Colorado trip. Victor, Dylynn and Ben arrived early to help with the wedding preparations. Hannah had everything well in hand so there wasn't much to do except my dress. I described what I was thinking to Dylynn and she thought she could manage it. I wanted flowing, floor-length pants that hung in a way that disguised the inseams so it looked like a skirt. The blouse would have a matching flow that gathered on the sides to create a rouched drape. I wasn't good at drawing, but I tried to sketch out what I had in my head. Luckily, Dylynn knew me well enough to know what I was trying to explain. She had me do a few fittings here and there. Otherwise, I left her to it. When she had me try it on after she finished, I couldn't believe how perfectly she'd recreated the vision I had. It was perfect. Pants that looked like a dress! I would be so much more comfortable on the wedding day.

I secreted in a pair of kid leather boots in a burnt amber color to wear with my pants-dress and an identical pair for Hannah made out of cream-colored calf skin. They wouldn't show under her dress, but I wanted her to have them for her day so I splurged.

I couldn't wait to give them to her, so I called her into my room the night they arrived. Her jaw dropped when she opened the box and she sat down on the floor to try them on right there. "Mom, they're perfect. It's like they've already been broken in and they were made for my feet! Thank you! They're going to pair well with my…dress." I caught the pause but let it go when she looked up at me with tears in her eyes. "What is it, Hannah?" Burying her face in her hand, she wept and I was terrified. "Hannah, honey. You have to tell me what's wrong. I can't help you if you won't tell me." Settling herself with a deep breath, I handed her a kerchief to dry her tears. Her chin quivered when she said, "I don't know how you've lived, Mom. I think about how much I need Josh and how excited I am for our future together, and I can't imagine being here without him. The thought of it physically makes me sick. How did you keep going after Dad died? I've always known you were strong but now that I know what you must have gone through and never showed it, I can't wrap my mind around what you're made of to manage it. I know you don't love Tyson. You've given Beau and I a perfect childhood and I'll never be able to thank you enough for it, but I don't think I could sacrifice myself like you have."

I slid down the wall and joined her on the floor. Pulling her to me, I held her in the quiet for several moments as I let the clock's ticking settle my heartbeat. "I didn't do it by myself, Hannah. God gave me the grace to get through every part of it; the bad days, the horrible days and the wonderful ones. I talk to your dad every day. If I'm not praying to God in my head, I'm talking to your dad in my heart. He was the light of my life, but he passed that on to you to help me get through this life without him. You have been the force that kept me going. When I get in the dark places, I look at you and see his eyes shining back at me. I hear him at night when I lie awake in bed. I talk to him out on the ridge when I need to center myself. I haven't gotten through it without him because I've never let him go. I keep him right beside me and I've poured all of the love he and I had for each other into you. Don't cry for me, Hannah. Your dad and I are going to be together again someday and then we'll have eternity. I don't want to leave you, but I know I have that day ahead. I've done my best to make him proud of us and I know he is. A lot of people never know what love is. My heart breaks for people in loveless marriages and I'll never stop being grateful that Josh came into your life. You two are going to have your own story and it's going to be magnificent." She nestled her head against my shoulder and asked, "Can you and Tyson both give me away on my wedding day? I don't feel right about Tyson doing it alone. I want you beside me because I know Dad will be standing there with you."

I kissed her on the temple and repeated the phrase I've said to her as many times as I could through the years, "Of course. Anything you want."

CHAPTER 37

Josh and Hannah's wedding day was a bright, crisp fall day. Mouthwatering aromas had been filling the house the last few days as Marta and Dylynn prepared all the food. All of Josh and Hannah's favorites were going to be set out on the buffet in the dining room, and Marta and Dylynn outdid themselves on the wedding cake; alternating layers of lemon and strawberry cake with Marta's special whipped frosting that Hannah had loved since she was a child.

Hannah chose swags made from leafy branches of the different trees found on the ranch and accented them with stalks of wheat to complement her fall-colored theme. Her taste was simple, but the dining room and porch décor were a testament to her classy style. When I was allowed entrance into her bedroom to help her get ready, we both gasped in unison, "You're wearing pants!" and hugged each other as we cackled. She was my daughter through and through. I should have known that's why she and Marta were keeping the wedding "dress" design to themselves. The cream silk jacquard artfully puffed at the shoulder and plunged just enough to hint at Hannah's décolletage without exposing too much. The waist was fitted and a wrap skirt draped open just enough to reveal the pants Marta had sewn into the dress. The pants tapered in just enough to fit over the calfskin boots I'd surprised Hannah with. She was a stunning bride and I couldn't take my eyes off her. Her hair was half up with loose curls framing her face and cascading down her back, and she tucked heads of wheat into her hair. I handed her a velvet box and said, "The boots are new and this should cover something old and borrowed." Hannah opened the jewel box and tears pooled in her eyes, "Gramma's pearls. Oh, Mom. I didn't even think about a necklace. Thank you, these are perfect. Will you help me put them on?" I took the string from her and fastened the clasp at the nape of her neck, "What about something blue?" Hannah winked at me as she lifted her pant leg up above her knee to showcase Josh's blue wild rag tied around her thigh like a garter. Chuckling, I told her she was a mess.

Marta and Dylynn went down to do one last check on the food and let everyone know we'd be starting soon. I hugged Hannah to me and choked out, "It's time for you to go find your own light, baby. I love you." I walked my Hannah down the stairs and out onto the back lawn where Tyson waited for us. He held out his arm for her and I held her hand as we went around the side of the house to the front steps, and then I gave my light into Josh Tanner's care.

It was a magical day. Hannah's attention to detail and Marta and Dylynn's fabulous food were the stuff dreams are made of. Beau stood up with Josh and they were so handsome standing on that porch when we came around the side of the house. Hannah had made wild rags out of my excess dress material and fashioned small lapel boutonnieres from a cluster of leaves with wheat stalks in the center for Josh and Beau. Their dark tan coats emphasized how their broad shoulders tapered down to trim waists. Victor had given all the gentlemen haircuts and everyone looked spectacular. Beau and I had been working on a surprise for the newlyweds' first night together. They thought they were going into town for a night at the hotel so they each had a bag ready. When it was time to go, Beau was supposed to pull the wagon around for them but came from the barn leading Josh and Hannah's horses instead. They looked questioningly at Beau. He smiled and looked at me, "Do you want to tell them?" I'd been keeping this quiet for so long. It was fun to finally let them in on our secret surprise. "Beau and I decided the cowboy shack on the south section needed to be fixed up. We're going to need to start using it again, and we thought you two could test it out to make sure it's comfy. I handed them their bags, "Tie your bags on and ride out. Stay as long as you like. We have things covered here until you're back."

THE LIGHT SEARCHER

We'd stocked it with all their favorite treats. I rode out early this morning with a block of ice for the ice box and filled it with champagne and some cheeses we'd special ordered. The fireplace was set and ready to light. Beau and I tried to think of everything they would need so it would be just right for them. From the looks they were sharing, I doubt they would notice any of the details of the cabin. I remembered my first night as Cal's wife and felt the stab in my heart that always came with the memories of our love. With hugs and goodbyes, we all cheered the newlyweds as they rode off.

I sat out on my porch long into the night bundled in a quilt and relived all the memories from my wedding night. I walked slowly through each part of the day in my mind, savoring the story of the day and saving the best part for last. Hot tears ran down my face when I opened my eyes to look up at the stars. Cal, I don't know how much longer I can be here without you. It's tearing me up inside.

CHAPTER 38

"I know talking about your parents hurts. I don't want you to hurt, but I do want to know who you come from, Josh." Lying on the rug in front of the fireplace, I asked Josh to tell me about his childhood, how he grew up, how he'd become so good with horses—everything. I wanted to know everything. Covering his eyes with his arm, he turned his head away from me. "I loved them, Hannah. I was their only child. Mom couldn't have any more after me. She never told me what was wrong, just that she wasn't able to have more children. I wondered what it would be like to have brothers and sisters, but Mom and Dad filled the hole as best they could. They were the kind of parents I want to be to our kids someday. I grew up watching them love each other and always felt loved by them. Mom was my playmate. She taught me how to cook and mend my clothes and Dad was the one who gave me my love of horses. He could walk into a round pen with a green colt and have it following him around like a lamb by the end of the day. You and your mom have a gift with horses, too. I love watching you work together. It reminds me of Dad and me. It doesn't hurt so much as it gnaws at my heart. The loneliness sits in my gut and burns when I watch you with your family. I wish so badly you could have known them. Mom was full of energy and bright. She smiled and laughed and her eyes twinkled when she looked at Dad." Hannah nodded, "I know that look. I have a picture in my head of Mom looking at Dad like that. Mom was at the stove cooking dinner. Dad came in from outside and smacked her on the rear. She leaned back into him and looked up at him with a twinkle in her eyes. I was so little, but I remember it clearly. Mom will never love again." Raising his head to look down at me, he questioned me, "You don't think she loves Tyson?" I shrugged and shook my head, "I don't think—I know. I remember what Mom and Dad were like. Mom isn't that way anymore. She's always put me first and then Beau after we moved here. Doing what was best for us kept her here and I know that's why she married Tyson. They've never shared a bedroom and Mom still wears the wedding ring Dad gave her. When she and Tyson married, he added a small band with diamonds on it but I see Mom pull them apart when she sits idle. She pulls the bands apart and twists Dad's ring around and around while she gazes off into nowhere. When I catch her like that, I can almost feel the heaviness she carries. She loves my dad and she always will. That kind of love doesn't make room for another." Cuddling me back into his chest, Josh whispered, "I get it. I didn't for a lot of years. Then I saw you walk out of the barn in pants that first day Beau hired me and I felt like I'd been struck by lightning. I love you, Hannah. The kind of love that doesn't leave room for another." As he stroked my hair back from my face, I sighed, "I wanted it. I wanted what Mom and Dad had but I didn't know if it would happen for me. I'm so glad you walked on our place, Josh. I'm so glad your steps brought you here. I hate that you had to lose your parents and leave the mountains you loved to get away from it, but I can't hate that your leaving brought you to me. I get this one life and I'm only going to live it with you."

CHAPTER 39

Tyson was a doting uncle to Ben as far as most on the ranch knew, but my guilt over the truth made me overly conscious of the attention Tyson paid him. Ben was devoted to Victor and tried to mimic him in every way. Whether it was his laugh or his gait, Ben was determined to be just like his father. I could see how it hurt Tyson in the smile that didn't quite go to his eyes. My anger over the situation had long since passed and with that peace came sympathy for Tyson's sadness over the consequences he and Dylynn had to live with for the rest of their lives.

Tyson was on all fours in the library giving pony rides to Ben. An excited Ben kicked at Tyson's sides to encourage the fun and had us all in stitches. Tyson tired easily and congratulated Ben on breaking his pony so quickly. To reward him for being such a good cowboy, Tyson convinced him to settle the horse into a trot that could be managed from Tyson's comfortable chair instead of the rough play on the floor. Ben relented and let Tyson gather him up for a bearhug as they moved to the chair where Tyson bounced Ben on his knee. I looked at Dylynn as the tender moment passed and she turned her eyes out the window pretending not to see my glance. Victor reached a hand toward her and lovingly rubbed her shoulder. The look of love that passed between them when she turned to Victor struck me unexpectedly and it was my turn to set my eyes on the horizon out the window while I swallowed the lump that had formed in my throat. I ached for that feeling again. I would move heaven and earth to have Cal's hand on my shoulder and share our intimacy with just a look between us.

Ben was played out and had leaned back against Tyson's chest with heavy lids. Dylynn walked over to the chair and softly nodded down at Tyson as she picked the sleepy boy up out of his embrace. The look of gratefulness and her nod said all the words Dylynn could not utter out loud. As she left the room with Ben, Victor rose from his seat. He stopped at Tyson's chair, laid a hand on Tyson's shoulder and held out his other hand to shake with Tyson's. One tear slipped from Tyson's eye and carried his remorse and regret down his cheek. Victor subtly shook his head as if to say, "No. Don't be sad. All is well." He gave Tyson's shoulder a squeeze and followed Dylynn to help put Ben down for the night.

Two days after Josh and Hannah's wedding, Tyson and I watched as Beau drove the wagon out of the yard with Victor, Dylynn and Ben. They were going home to Colorado and Beau was taking them to catch their train. As we'd said our goodbyes and given our last hugs for this trip, Tyson held his bearhug with Ben until he squirmed. With a chuckle, he set him up in the wagon with Victor and tousled his hair. The question in Beau's eyes didn't go unnoticed by me, but he never brought it up after he returned from dropping them at the train station. Fortunately, Ben had taken after Dad and shared Dylynn's features rather than Tyson's. It was a saving grace in our attempt to keep Ben's biological father a secret.

Later that evening while Tyson and I worked on the books in the office, I spoke my thoughts. "Tyson, you are going to have to figure out how to mask the love you have for Ben in front of Beau and the hands. Beau can read people like a book—especially you. With you, I swear sometimes he knows your thoughts before you do. You need to be careful if you intend to keep this from him for the rest of his life." He stared through me without seeing me and I could tell he was lost in whatever was going on in his head. He'd heard me, though. His distant voice was wracked with conflicting emotions when he replied, "I want Beau to know. I asked Dylynn if we could sit down with him and explain, but she was adamant that we keep this between us as we agreed. Victor is Ben's father, and she doesn't want to disrespect that by bringing Beau into it. It feels wrong to deprive him of his brother, but it's not fair of me to ask that of Victor. We promised we'd take this to the grave and Dylynn begged me to honor my promise. I can't tell him and it's breaking me, Beth. No, it's not breaking me. It has broken me and I won't recover."

CHAPTER 40

We sorted sick cattle and kept them in separate pens away from the herd. Beau doctored them each day until he decided they were fit enough to rejoin the herd. We had a cow getting ready to calf that we were watching. She'd lost her first calf so we wanted to make sure everything went alright with this one. I'd been out on the ridge this morning and noticed the windmill wasn't pumping. When I got back to the barn, I went in search of Beau to let him know he needed to send someone out to fix it. When I got to the pen, Beau and Matthew were arguing.

The cow had calved another stillborn and then prolapsed. She was getting rough with the calf to rouse it and Beau needed to settle her to get her pushed back in. "Matthew! Rope her and pull her up to the fence or we'll lose them both!" Matthew stood on the bottom rail of the fence ready to jump if the cow came near him. "You can't fix a prolapse, Beau. You've already lost them both. Just let me go get the gun and we'll put her down." Beau dodged a horn the cow speared his direction and tried to get between the cow and calf, "We're not putting her down. I can fix the prolapse, but I need your help. You're living off us for free. The least you could do is help save this cow. If we can fix the prolapse, we can ship her this summer for the beef. This is money we'd be wasting. Rope her now before she kills me!" Matthew threw his leg over the fence and hopped down on the other side. "You're an idiot, kid. I'm going to get the gun."

I'd run back into the barn for a rope while Matthew bucked Beau, but I heard the whole thing. Meeting Matthew with a scowl on my face as he traipsed back to the barn at a stroll, I ran up to the fence. I stood up on the rail and braced myself with my legs, looped the cow's horns, hopped back down and pulled the rope over the fence to hold her. Looping my end around a post for leverage, I pulled her up to the fence and let her settle while Beau carried the calf out of the pen. Tying off the rope to hold the cow still, I asked Beau what he needed. "There's a bag over here on the other side of the gate. Just hand it over to me." Beau deftly repaired the damaged womb and had the cow intact quickly. He said we'd need to keep her calm and still for a few days until he could put her back in the pasture. Just leave her tied for a bit. Let's take care of this calf and we'll come back to check on her. Beau gathered his tools and I carried his bag as we walked back to the tack room. Matthew walked toward us with the gun and Beau stopped him, "You are here because of some history with my dad that none of us knows about. I can't do anything about that, but hear me: The day I can do something about it, you will be gone. Until then, don't you ever walk away from me when I've asked for your help. You are the man who lives in the manager's house but you do not manage this ranch." I stood by Beau as Matthew seethed. I didn't like the look in his eyes while he held a gun in his hands, but Beau was unaffected by the threat. Over his shoulder as he walked away from us, Matthew said, "That cow won't make it. They can't live through a prolapse. Mark my words."

Beau and I cleaned up his kit, buried the calf and then went to check the cow. Beau told me to give her some slack a little at a time. She let us release her and stayed calm, but the minute she had enough room she started butting the rails of the pen. Calves of other cows were bawling nearby and Beau thought we should move her to the other side of the barn in hopes that being further away would calm her and keep her still until she was healed. It took Beau, Hannah, Josh and me to get her moved to the quieter side, and she nearly took Beau out twice before we got her there. The four of us were back in the barn when I told Beau about the pump on the windmill. He said he'd have someone check it tomorrow morning. Matthew was leaning on the barn with one foot propped up against the side right outside the door when we walked out.

Chewing on a toothpick, he challenged Beau with a glance. Beau said, "Ride out to the windmill to check that pump tomorrow morning. The cattle on that piece can't be without water." Matthew straightened and brushed off his sleeves as he responded sardonically, "You ride out there and check that pump. I'm just the man who lives in the manager's house. I'm not the manager."

CHAPTER 41

I wondered how the cow had done through the night so I went to the barn to find Beau for a report. He was nowhere in the barn and not in the pens so I suspected he was checking the cow on the other side. Nearing the pens, I saw Beau's hat over the fence rails. He was standing in the pen across from the cow to look in on her. As I walked toward the pen, I saw Matthew slipping through the alley on the other side. I came around the corner just as Matthew opened the gate to the prolapsed cow's pen and slapped her rear to startle her. She burst through the alley into the pen where Beau was standing. I didn't want to raise my voice in case it upset the angry cow more so I ran to the open gate. The cow snorted and bellowed while she pawed the ground. Beau lay in a heap in the corner of the pen, but I couldn't see well enough to see how badly he was injured. I opened both gates and hollered to get the cow moving back into her pen. Once she was through, I slammed her gate shut and ran to Beau. He was too still. "Beau! How bad are you hurt?" I went to him to sit him up and fell to my knees, "No! Not you, Beau. You were so good. Not my Beau!"

Josh, Hannah and the hands around the barn heard my howls and came running. Josh sprung into action and laid Beau out to see how badly he was hurt. Hannah held me as I rocked and assured me Josh could help. I shook my head back and forth over and over. I knew there was nothing Josh could do. Angry longhorn cattle were dangerous and we all respected that. This was why. The cow had run straight at Beau when Matthew startled her and she gored him. Beau was gone.

I searched for Matthew and found him nowhere. Giving up, I headed to the house to get Tyson and found him in the office with Matthew. I lunged at him, "You killed my boy! Get off this ranch!" But Tyson's voice thundered back "BETH! What on earth is wrong with you? Matthew's been in here with me." I went for him again, but Tyson wrapped his arm around my waist to restrain me. "You opened that gate and put that mad cow on Beau. You knew exactly what would happen and I saw you do it. Don't you dare deny it!" Matthew dismissed me with a laugh as if I were delusional, "Tyson, I don't know who she saw, but it wasn't me. I came straight here this morning from my house." I looked at Tyson and he shook his head at me. "Beth, I know you don't care for Matthew but this is a serious accusation. Is Beau alright? What happened?" I wilted to the floor in tears, "He killed our boy, Tyson. He let that cow into the pen with Beau and she gored him. He's gone!" Tyson fell back in his desk chair and laid his head on his desk. Deep groaning turned to wails. We sat there, Tyson with his head on his desk and me in a heap on the floor, weeping for our Beau. Again, Matthew slipped away unnoticed.

CHAPTER 42

We buried Beau in the family cemetery beside his mother and walked back down to the house. Marta prepared a meal, but I couldn't eat. I went to my room and stayed there the rest of the day. The next morning, Tyson knocked on my door, "Beth? Are you awake?" I groaned an exhausted yes. "Will you come to the office when you get around? I need to speak to you." The office? We put our boy in the ground yesterday and he wants me in the office today? I shot out of bed in pure anger and jerked on my clothes.

Tyson was at his desk when I walked in and I glared at him. "What could possibly be so important that we're required to be in the office first thing this morning, and why aren't you looking for Matthew?" He was failing and it was visible. His frame was thin where it used to be muscular and his skin maintained a yellowish pallor. He could barely saddle his own horse anymore, much less work a full day with the hired hands. He'd been spending most of his days in the office so I'd been avoiding him at all costs. It was just better for my peace that I steer clear of Tyson when I could.

He looked at me with pleading eyes and asked me to sit down. His tone was odd and I was wary of the conversation he wanted to have. I took a seat across from him and waited for him to speak. "Matthew's gone. I have hands out looking for him with strict orders to bring him back here when they find him. I doubt they will, though." He buried his face in his hands before he began again, "Beth, I don't know how much longer I have. We're grief-stricken and this is a horrible time, but I have to set this right as soon as possible. I don't want to take any chances that it isn't taken care of before I pass. I left the ranch to Beau. He loved you like a mother and I knew he would always be fair to you, so I wasn't concerned about you being cared for after I'm gone. With Beau passing, I want to update my will. I've rewritten my wishes. It's all here for you and Hannah. I'm leaving the ranch here to Hannah and the Colorado ranch will remain Ben's inheritance as we've always planned. Before I call Hannah in here, I wanted to let you know my thoughts."

I scoffed, "Thank you for letting me know your thoughts. Will that be all?" He looked pained, "I thought you'd be thrilled. Are you angry?" Was I angry? After a calming breath, I answered, "Angry. I've worked so hard to find my peace after the unfairness this world has dealt me, and I've chosen light so many times when darkness would have been easier. I've covered your lies, I've lived with Matthew Bishop being on this place, and I've been here with your son while you chose to go haunt Victor and Dylynn just to watch Ben grow up. I've worked this ranch like it's my own and you don't ask me about this before you decide it's done. You just allow me the kindness of knowing what you're doing before you tell Hannah. That's gentlemanly of you, Tyson. You don't think I could've run this ranch and passed it on to Hannah? You just assume you're doing me a favor by giving it directly to her? Can you not see how that is a slap in my face for everything I've withstood from you?

"Honestly, I am thrilled you're passing it down to Hannah and Josh. They will continue your legacy and make it even more than we have. I guess I should just be thanking the heavens you didn't run us all off and leave it to Bishop."

He hung his head. "I thought this would be what you wanted. I'm sorry. I feel like all I've done is tell you how sorry I am for the last fifteen years. When does my penance end, Beth?"

I stood over his desk so I was looking down on him, "There it is. You think you're the one who's suffered all these years. That's how selfish and small you are. Please leave the ranch to Hannah with my blessing. She will make us both proud. I will go ask her to join us so you can give her the news."

CHAPTER 43

Tyson went to his room after talking to Hannah and he never left it. The next morning, he didn't come down for breakfast. I knocked on his door and heard his raspy, "Come in." He was still in bed and his pallor was worse. "What time is it, Beth? I'm so tired." Setting his nightstand clock so he could see it, I said, "It's 9:00 in the morning, Tyson." He struggled to prop himself up on his pillows, so I helped him sit up. "Beth," he wheezed, "I can't get up. Could you ask Marta to bring me a tray?" I straightened his covers and went back to the door, "I'll bring you a tray. Is there anything else?" He coughed weakly and asked me to bring the file on his desk with the tray.

I poked my head into the kitchen to ask Marta for a breakfast tray and went on to the office. When I picked up the file Tyson asked for, a tattered document slipped out and slid across the floor. I could make out Tyson's penmanship. It looked like a contract. I opened it and dropped onto the couch in disbelief.

It was written like a receipt and signed by both parties, Tyson Bauer and Matthew Bishop. There were several loose check stubs inside the folded contract.

For services rendered
Sand-Rich Stockyards sale
$2,000.00

Forgetting the tray, I stormed up to Tyson's room with the vague contract and check stub crumpled in my hand. I threw the wadded paper at him and quietly demanded, "Tell me everything."

Tyson caved in on himself and sobbed. I leaned toward him, "You don't get to do this now. What did you do, Tyson?" He took a steadying breath and confessed a darkness so black, I wouldn't recover.

"Matthew and I met in Dalhart after I left the bank one day to deposit the money from a cattle shipment. He struck up a conversation with me at the restaurant in the hotel that evening and I invited him to have dinner with me. He told me about a stockyard that could be for sale in Nebraska soon if things didn't turn around for the owners. I was looking for investments and I knew the Nebraska cattle market was bound to come back soon, so I was intrigued. Matthew convinced me he could persuade the owners to sell once they had no other choice. It was just a matter of time. I told him to set a meeting and I would travel to Ogallala to discuss the purchase with the owners when the time was right. We signed a contract that night ensuring he would receive a headhunter's fee for bringing me the opportunity and setting up the sale.

Later, he wrote to me detailing the turn of events that had taken place at Sand-Rich and that the owners were going to save the business by diversifying into horse sales. They were breaking colts and selling them to ranchers and cowboys who traveled through Ogallala. They were turning a good profit and it looked like they would be able to maintain the stockyards until cattle got good again. I thanked Matthew for trying, sent him a check for his trouble for $200 and told him I was interested in other opportunities if he found anything else. I thought our business was over. Months later, he wired me to let me know the owners had changed their mind and I should come to Nebraska to start negotiations. I told him when I planned to be there and he scheduled the meeting for me. It was just days later I heard the news of the fire at the stockyards and that there had been a fatality. I wired Matthew to ask if all was well. He responded that the sale was incentivized and the meeting was still on. When I received his response that used the word "incentivized," I knew I wanted no part of whatever was going on and wired him that the sale was off.

He turned up in Dalhart a few weeks later with his wife and demanded I see him. He showed up here at the ranch and insisted I go through with the deal and that I owed him at least that for working the situation to my benefit. Before he arrived, the news had been around that you were widowed from the death at the stockyards. I was tortured thinking about having anything to do with your demise so I placed the ad in the paper and prayed it would be a lifeline for you and your daughter. My intention was to right a horrible wrong. I tried to run Matthew off, but he threatened to expose my involvement and tell the authorities I hired him to burn your horse barn. I paid him to stay away for years until the day he turned back up here. His wife had passed and he was broke. He told me if I'd hire him as ranch manager, he wouldn't go to the authorities. I couldn't take the chance of you finding out. I promise you, Beth. I never asked Matthew to burn that barn. My intentions were only to invest in the stockyards if you were willing to sell. I rue the day I met that man and I've been trying to take care of you ever since to help myself live with what happened to you. Forgive me, Beth. I need to hear you say you forgive me."

I leaned back in the chair beside his bed and stared at the wall, "Tyson, forgiveness is the only thing that has kept me sane all these years. Even when I didn't feel forgiving, I just kept asking God to help me forgive you. For all of the wrongs you tried to right, I thank you. For doing right by Dylynn and Ben, I thank you. But forgiving you for Cal's death, I cannot do because you aren't to blame. Matthew Bishop killed Cal, not you."

Tyson tried to move toward me and coughed violently. Blood flew onto the bedspread and Tyson fell back on his pillows. "Tyson!" I cried out his name as his eyelids fluttered. I tried to clean his chin and he reached for my hand. He struggled to get air and his voice was faint. "He's dangerous, Beth. He'll try to come back. I can't protect you anymore." His grip on my hand loosened and his arm fell slack to his chest.

CHAPTER 44

Tyson was right. That night after Tyson passed, Matthew walked in the back door and came through the kitchen like he owned the place. I was in the library when Marta ran in behind him. "I'm sorry, Beth. He just came right in." I nodded at her, "It's fine, Marta. Mr. Bishop isn't staying."

After Marta left the room, I turned on Matthew, "How dare you walk into my home uninvited? Much less show your face at this ranch after what you've done?" He chuckled and sat on the duvet, "Funny thing about that, Beth. I hear this isn't your house anymore. I hear it's Hannah's. Now, she wouldn't turn out her poor old Uncle Matthew, would she?"

Walking right up to him so he had to look up at me, I rounded with, "Hannah despises you as much as Beau and I did. She won't have you on this ranch." He shrugged and grinned, "I don't see it that way. The way I figure it, Tyson owes me this ranch for everything he put me through." I couldn't contain the hysteria his deranged comment dredged up out of me. Laughing, I rallied, "Owes you? Tyson owes you nothing. We know the truth about you. Tyson bore his soul right before he passed. I know every sordid detail; the lies, the bribery and the murders!" The slimy grin was wiped away and cool evil filled Matthew's eyes, "You've known me long enough to know that people who get in the way of what I want tend to meet an untimely demise. I'm surprised you have the bravado to speak to me in that manner when I could so easily remove you, Hannah and Josh right out of my way. No one would think the wiser. My good friend Tyson wrote it into his will that should all descendants be departed, the ranch would turn over to me." He pulled a document out of his coat pocket and handed it to me. It was a forged will. I had to give it to him, he'd perfected Tyson's signature. Before he could unplant himself from his seat, I hurried to the fireplace and threw the fake will in the flames. Lurching to his feet, he rushed to the fire to retrieve the papers but they were already too far gone. "Get out of my house. Get off this ranch. If you ever see me again, I will be the last thing you see before I send you to burn, Matthew Bishop." His sinister laugh drifted back to me as he left the house through the back door.

CHAPTER 45

Within a week, we buried both Bauer men. Josh braced Hannah up as they placed Tyson's coffin in the ground beside the fresh mound of raw earth that was Beau's grave. I was breaking for her. My poor precious girl had suffered so much loss. All I ever wanted was to give her the world, and I was devastated that I couldn't protect her from this pain.

As we turned back toward the house, I looked out toward the ridge and saw Matthew riding in that direction. Where had he come from? What on earth was he doing here? I settled Hannah in the house with Josh and changed into riding clothes. I stepped into the library to tell Josh I was going for a ride and my heart caught. Josh was sitting on the couch with Hannah curled up beside him. She'd cried herself to sleep on his chest and he was holding her while she rested. I pointed to the barn and mouthed that I was going riding. Josh nodded gently and I blew them a kiss. Holding my hand to my heart, I whispered, "I love you both so much."

I took my time getting to my spot on the ridge. I just wanted to be alone with my thoughts and Cal. I had to find Matthew and figure out how to get him to leave us alone. If it was money, we could pay him. But would he ever really go away? Pulling up my horse near a sage brush that overlooked the windmill, I spotted Matthew working at the base to fix the pump. He has truly convinced himself this ranch will be his. If he's hiding out around here, he's planning something. What if he hurts Josh and Hannah? I heard Cal on the wind the same as I did the day I came out here to talk to him about Hannah marrying Josh, "It's time, Beth." Yes, it was time—time to end the evil this man carried inside him.

I didn't hesitate. Josh would always take care of Hannah. This ranch would be their legacy, they would thrive and I would make sure of it. I stood there staring at him as he worked and a calm fell over me. I sent my parting words to him on the wind that blew down from the ridge. "I vowed to protect Beau and Hannah. I failed Beau but you won't ever touch Hannah." I held my rifle up to settle the scope on him and took a breath. I squeezed the trigger on my exhale and felt a hammer blow to my left hip as the shot rang out. The rattler had been hiding in the shade of the sage bush next to me and the shot startled it into striking. Searing pain shooting up into my torso doubled me over as the snake disappeared into the rocks a few feet away. Moments ago, my blood coursed through me as I accepted my duty to secure Josh and Hannah's safety. Now, I can feel my slowing heartbeat. Lying at the edge of the ridge in the quiet of my last breaths, my eyes searched for the body next to the windmill. Matthew's dead gaze was all I needed to confirm Hannah would be free to live her life without the threat of his malice. I closed my eyes and the light faded. My soul left my body to begin its journey back to Cal.

CHAPTER 46

Sounds of water drifting over smooth stones soothed me as I traveled the path beside the winding creek. Warm sunlight touched my back as my gaze went to our house up on the rise. Exquisite golden light was on everything and in everything. Cal was coming down the hill and the light was all around him. He held his arms out to me and I ran to him. He cradled my head with his strong hand and kissed me. As I leaned back to drown in his eyes, the light filled me and we were both luminous. "I've waited so long for this, Cal. I did my best, but I couldn't be there anymore without you." He pulled me back to his chest and held me there, "You're here, Beth. You're in the light now and it's all that matters. The others will be along in time. Welcome home."